Alina

Shayna Astor

Edited by NiceGirlNaughtyEdits
Edited by Beth Hudson
Cover Designer Fine's Fine Designs
Formatting Fine's Fine Designs

Alina

Copyright © 2023 Shayna Astor

From the Author

Alina is a full-length, novel that features strong language, mature situations, explicit sexual scenes, alcohol use, mentions of death, grieving, addiction, cancer, and loss from cancer. This book is intended for readers age 18 and up.

While Alina can be read as a stand alone, it is recommended to read the series in order.

Thank you so much for reading my novel! I hope you enjoy reading it, as much as I enjoyed writing it!

Other Books by Shayna Astor

Hot & Cold

Shattered Pieces

Own Me (A dark romance)

Off Limits (Book 1 in the Limits Series)

Love Me Not

Faking Perfection: A Brighton High School Reunion

Dedication

To giving second chances and allowing people the room
to grow and change.

Chapter 1
Alina

Laughter fills the otherwise quiet café as Liv has me gripping my sides. She's always been able to make me see the light, to find the good in the bad. I know it's not that way for her, but she can do it for me. And it makes me love her all the more. She may be my sister, but she's also my best friend.

When she suddenly stops, all color draining from her face and her mouth hanging open, my heart crashes to the ground. Something bad is happening behind me, and I'm scared to turn around.

"Hey, Liv." *That voice.*

Now her expression makes sense.

"You have a lot of nerve coming in here like everything is fine, Cameron." Her tone is stern as she speaks for me.

I flinch at the mention of his name. Instead of turning around, I place a hand on Liv's arm, drawing her attention, and lightly tilt my head toward the kitchen. My safe place, my solace.

She gives the slightest nod, and I walk away, every move I make to avoid seeing him. Because as much as I tell myself I've moved on, that

I've forgotten about him, the scars on my heart ache at the deep timber of his voice.

"Alina." My shoulders hunch as my name rolls off his tongue. I used to love the way he said it, the way he could make it sound like the sweetest song. Now, it only brings me pain.

"Don't you dare talk to her." It's the last thing I hear as I disappear through the door to the kitchen.

Once through it, my hand flies to my chest and I try to gulp down air. My heart is pounding against my sternum, and I can't take a deep breath no matter how hard I try.

"Leen?" Liv pokes her head in right as I double over, one hand on my knee while the other tries to contain my heart. "Oh, Alina." Her arm drapes over my shoulder and she pulls me into her side.

"What...is he...doing here?"

"Well, he's not here anymore. I made sure of that. But I don't know. He said he wanted to see you, that he's back." Back? What does that mean? For good? For the day?

"Why?"

"Your guess is as good as mine. He may have been like another brother to me, but you were obviously a lot closer with him." At one point, I was pretty sure he *would* be a brother to her. We were so set, so strong, I was positive we were going to get married. That all changed when he left.

"I can't handle him being back, Liv."

"Listen, I know he was your first love, your big love, but you've moved on. Right? You've dated. Hell, you were with Sean for two years."

Sean was just a bandage on a gaping wound. Yes, he was sweet and kind and wanted to be with me, but his love never had a chance to compare to what I had with Cameron once upon a time.

"It's not about moving on, Liv, and it's not about still having feelings for him. He *broke* me when he left. It took far too long for me to heal from that. Nothing good can come from him being back. There's nothing left between us, no torches held. It's just going to stir up bad feelings. It already is."

Tipping my head back against the door, I stare at the ceiling, willing away the torrent of tears threatening to fill my eyes. It's been ten years since Cameron left. I've moved on, I've dated, even came close to getting engaged once. But the way he left, the memories, the times we shared, seeing him again, hearing his voice, has torn open those wounds.

He was everything to me for so many years. We may have been young, only eighteen when he left, but we were so in love. Nothing has quite compared. And I was okay with that. I've come to terms with the fact that I may never find somebody who makes me feel the way Cameron did.

"Why is he here, Liv?" The thought is going to plague my mind for as long as he's around.

"I don't know. Maybe to see his folks? Aren't they still local?"

"Yeah, but has he not seen them in ten years? I can't imagine that's the case. He has to have been coming back here for years and made sure to stay hidden. Why now?" What's changed? Is it something about being a decade? Is there some sort of reunion I'm not aware of that he's here for and wanted to see me before being around all those people?

There has to be a reason and it can't just be to upturn my life. I've already let him do that once. I can't let him do it again.

"I couldn't tell you, Leen. Really. I wish I knew, that I had some sort of information or inkling, but I don't. All I know is that he seemed adamant. He said he'd be back."

"Fuck my life. I'm never leaving this kitchen again." And I'd gladly stay here forever. I can sleep on the benches; I don't need to be home. Maybe the nightmares will abate when I'm in my happy place.

But is it still happy, knowing he's going to be out there waiting?

My fingers tingle at my sides with the need to move, to do something, to *cook*. "I'm going to whip up some muffins."

"Leen, don't get too crazy."

"I won't, Sibby." Using Liv's long-standing nickname brings me a sense of comfort that I desperately want right now. "I just...I need to do something. You know that nervous energy."

"Want to stay at my place tonight?" She's anticipating a nightmare from his return. It's not the craziest thought because I wouldn't be surprised if I had one.

"No. I'll be fine. I don't want to impose on you and Jameson. He's been kind enough to share you if I have a nightmare. I don't need to stay with you too."

"Well, if this stirs up any memories or bad dreams, you just let me know. Don't hesitate to call."

I glance at her and don't answer.

She takes my shoulders in her hands and turns me to face her. "He may be my husband, but you are my sister, and I love you. If you need me, you are to call me so I can be there for you. Understood?"

I can't meet her gaze, but I nod as I stare down at the tiled floor beneath our feet. It makes me feel so weak that I lose such control of my mind while I'm asleep. I'd rather just not sleep. And I do try, but eventually, my body fails me, and I pass out.

Jameson tried to have a conversation with me, urging me to seek help. But I can't trust a stranger with my problems.

In fact, I have a hard time trusting anybody, and a large reason for that is because of the man who just stopped into my café entirely uninvited.

With a squeeze of my shoulders, Liv walks back through the swinging door and out to the floor. It's almost lunchtime, which is always busy.

The second she's gone, I straighten up and do what I do best. Put Cameron out of my mind and focus on baking.

Chapter 2

Cameron

I knew coming back would be hard. But I had no idea The Bakers would make it *this* impossible. I've been here for three weeks, going into the café every day. And still, I have yet to see Alina for any more than a quick glimpse of her chocolate curls. Her warm caramel eyes are still emblazoned in my mind, but I know I'll be caught dead in my tracks when I finally see them.

"Let me see her, Liv." It's been the exact same begging from me every time. I can't keep pleading with the baby Baker. I need the real deal. Hell, even give me Mazie just for a change of pace. Though on second thought, maybe not. She scares me.

"Olivia. And why should I?"

"I've known you for years, Liv, why am I suddenly getting 'Olivia'?" She was a little girl in braided pigtails the first time I met her. Not that I was much older, but she seemed like such an innocent child. I quickly learned she was the roughest of the bunch.

"You've been *gone* for years, Cameron. That's why. Only my friends and siblings can call me Liv. That doesn't include you anymore." Her arms are crossed firmly over her chest. I know the stance a little too well.

I open my mouth to respond, but before I can, we're joined by a man who wraps his arm around Liv and pulls her into his side. She leans in with ease, loosening slightly, but keeping her arms crossed and eyes shooting daggers straight at me.

"Everything okay here?" His voice is deep and filled with authority. He's clearly something to Liv with the way she's leaning into him.

"Yes, he was just leaving." She doesn't take her eyes off me as she tells me what I'll be doing.

"Actually, I'm waiting for Alina." I'm trying my damnedest here to get just a few minutes.

"I told you, she's not coming out." The words come out through gritted teeth, and I know Liv is losing her patience with me, but what she wants me to do about it, I don't know. I came here for one thing and one thing only. That's Alina.

Out of the corner of my eye, I can see this guy, who seems to be some sort of boyfriend to Liv, looking back and forth between us, clearly trying to figure out what the fuck is going on and who I am. Possibly how I know either of them.

Trying to break the tension, or at least that's what I'm assuming, new guy tightens his grip on Liv and extends a hand in my direction.

"Hi. I'm Jameson."

"Cameron." I place my hand in his and meet his eyes. We're basically the same height, though I can imagine he tries to use it as an intimidation factor with others. But what intimidates me is his appearance. The expensive suit aside, he's very put together. And while I'm doing my best these days, I'm definitely not.

It takes me the extra second of giving him a once-over to notice the rather large sparkling diamond on Liv's left ring finger, which is now resting against this guy's chest.

Clearing my throat, I jut my chin toward the pair. "Congratulations."

Liv turns her head away, facing the wall and gripping Jameson's shirt. "Thanks, man. Listen, I don't know what's going on here, but you're upsetting my girl, and I can't have that right now."

"I know, I'm sorry. I'll go. Liv, please, tell Alina I'll be back tomorrow. And the next day. I'll be back every single day until she talks to me." Just like I have been every day for three weeks. And I'll keep coming back as long as it takes.

When she flips around, the hot pink streaks flying around her face, there's nothing but pure fury burning in her eyes. Instead of the violet they've always resembled, they somehow almost look red. "She's never going to talk to you, Cameron. You should just go back to wherever you came from. She's moved on, and she's not interested."

"Five minutes, Liv. All I need is five minutes." I bring my hands together in prayer, ready to get down on my knees and worship the ground she walks on for just five minutes with her sister.

"Good luck with that." Pushing off of Jameson, who tries to keep his grasp on her, she disappears through the same swinging door I know Alina's been parked behind this whole time.

Jameson looks back and forth between the kitchen and me, his face tight but softening. "What can I do to help you out?"

"I just need five minutes to talk to her. That's it." If she'd just give me some time to explain. It won't take more than a few minutes to go over what happened all those years ago, and then she's free to continue hating me if she needs to.

"Listen, I don't know who you are, what your deal is, but I know with these girls it can be tough to break through their defenses. Trust me. I'll see if there's anything I can do." The way he says "trust me," I know he's had his run in. Likely with Mazie, who's overly protective, especially of Liv.

I already like this guy. Eli would have chased me out with a shotgun the second he saw me. Zach would have intimidated me with his size and badge. But this new guy, he'll help me out. Probably because he doesn't know the history here, but that seems to be working in my favor right now, so who am I to question it.

My eyes are glued to the swinging black door when Jameson clears his throat. "Tell the girls I'll be back tomorrow. All I want is five minutes of Alina's time. That's it."

"I'll tell them."

I give him a curt nod and back out of the café. Tomorrow. I'll be back tomorrow. And every day after until Alina finally gives me five minutes. That's all I need to set things straight and start working toward getting her back.

Chapter 3
Alina

C ameron has kept good on his word about coming back repeatedly. He's been here *every single day*. The good thing is he doesn't hang around. At first, I was worried he'd wait for me to leave at night or surprise me in the morning, but he never has. At least, not so far.

He comes, Liv deals with him as he says his piece, and then he leaves. Every day is the same, even the same time.

The problem is that I'm letting him win. In a way. His goal is to talk to me, but instead, I'm letting him chase me away. I need to be strong. I need to let him see that he has no effect on me at all. Whatever happened a decade ago is just that. Ancient history.

So what if the nightmares returned after he left and never really abated? That at this point, they've stolen a piece of me? So what if he smashed my heart to smithereens? It's been a decade and most people move on after that much time.

He surely has.

And what's more? It's killing me not knowing why he's here or what he wants. For all I know, he wants to propose to somebody, but needs to clear some air between us. We never technically broke up, not that I'd still consider us dating after ten years of radio silence.

The curiosity is going to get the better of me. Liv has tried asking about a dozen times, but he refuses to speak to anybody but me.

The problem? I never stopped caring about him and wondering what the hell happened between us. For years, I've blamed myself. He was just gone without a word one day, never to be heard from again. It was almost like he never existed, except he'd left his mark all over me, mainly on my heart.

Even though I've tried to get past it, to make everything go away and to forget about him, I've never truly been able to. His blue-green eyes have haunted me for years. It's something I've resigned myself to, a life of comparing other men to Cameron, my first and truest love. If there's another that's truer than him, I have yet to meet that person. But I've also stopped looking.

It became too difficult to explain the nightmares, too much to keep giving so much of myself for so little in return. Too much to keep diving into the story of my childhood. Every new person required doing it over and over. After Cameron, I avoided dating anybody who lived in this town. It was too small, too claustrophobic. And there was too much pity that came along with dating a Baker.

Then there's Cameron, who knows the story on a personal level because he lived through that hell with me. He was there every second, every step of the way, until he wasn't.

Nobody else will have that bond with me. Nobody will have the firsthand experience and knowledge of what those days were like.

Despite all that happened with Cameron and his disappearance and the ache that it left in my soul, there's an undeniable connection that he and I will always have.

I'm sure he knows that, and I'm fairly confident he's counting on me being unable to deny it so that eventually I'll come out of the kitchen and face him.

It's been over three weeks of this, and he has yet to stop coming by. Thankfully, he's started being a patron too, getting a coffee and pastry during each visit.

I've had Liv pay close attention to what sort of pastry he orders. I'm trying to learn about him without talking to him, to see if his tastes and preferences are still the same.

From the intel I've been able to gather, coffee cake still reigns supreme, and he'll choose it over any other kind of muffin or scone. But there's a special muffin I make with fresh caramel on the inside. I don't make them often because they're a giant pain in the ass, having to make the caramel from scratch.

But I'm in the process right now. I got in early today thanks to lack of sleep. Not necessarily a nightmare, just a fitful night. I decided I had to try this experiment.

Caramels are his favorite candy, and he'll always go for anything caramel.

At least, the Cameron I knew would. It's a little test to see if I still know him. Why I care, I don't know, but something deep down inside me does. It's almost like I need to know that everything we had was real at some point, that the things I think I know about him, or knew at one point, were true.

So today I'm making muffins with a gooey caramel center. They're probably more akin to a cupcake but calling them a muffin seems more breakfast appropriate.

While I have zero intentions of leaving my safe haven, I'll ask Liv to pay close attention. She will, just because she always has my back, but she'll surely roll her eyes at me.

My curiosity with Cameron is something she doesn't condone, and I know that's partially because she's overprotective of me in a way only a sister can be.

As far as she's concerned, he hurt me and he's done, he's gone, he's out of my life.

Unfortunately, it's not seeming to be quite so simple.

Chapter 4
Cameron

Another day, another trip to Three Sticks Café. At this point, I'm convinced I might die before I get a chance to actually talk to Alina, but it's a risk I'm willing to take.

I haven't had another run-in with Jameson, and so far, Mazie hasn't come with her horns out. I'm fearfully awaiting that one.

It must mean I'm not bothering the girls *too* much.

"Hello, Olivia."

"Cameron." This is the most of a greeting I get out of her. It spoken in a cold and flat tone, but at least it's an acknowledgment of my existence.

"Is Alina here?"

She crosses her arms over her chest and tips her chin up. It's the same look I've gotten every day for three and a half weeks.

"She is, but she's not coming out. You should just stop this, Cameron. She's not going to talk to you. You're wasting your time coming here every day."

"Oh, nonsense. I get good coffee, delicious pastries, and your delightful disposition." I plaster a smile on my face. I like Liv; she's probably my favorite sibling. Eli used to be like a brother to me, but Liv is spunky and protective, and I appreciate that.

My joke has no effect on Liv, who grimaces instead of even contemplating a smirk. "She's not coming out, Cameron."

"So you've said. But I'll keep coming back until she does." I take a moment to peruse the pastry case and find something different this time. There's a chocolate muffin that's filled with caramel.

A smile breaks across my face. She may not be coming out to talk to me, but she's trying to tell me something. Or figure something out.

Alina knows caramel is my favorite and I'll always choose it. This is a test.

"Can I have the chocolate caramel muffin and a large black coffee, please. Don't worry. I'll take it to go."

Though it's brief, I don't miss the quick glance Liv makes at the kitchen door. This test is one I'm going to pass.

It's clear what this is about. She's trying to gauge if she still knows me. It may have been a decade since we've been together, but at one point, I knew Alina better than anybody.

There's a curiosity that has to be stirring inside her, at least a little bit. She has to be wondering what I'm doing back, all of a sudden, after ten years. Why now?

It's what I'd be asking if the tables were turned.

And it's not like I've never been back, I've just stayed hidden. It was an intentional choice I made to stay away from the café and Alina and the whole family, really. It was risky, and I haven't come back much, but I also haven't been terribly far.

I'm just over the border in Crucible County. At first, I stayed away because I knew she had to be furious. Then, I didn't know what to say.

Fuck, I still don't know what to say to her. But not a single damn day has gone by that I haven't thought about her.

That's a lot of time to think about somebody in such an unrequited way. Finally, I got up the nerve to come back and talk to her.

Plus, Mom needs me closer than an hour and a half away. Her treatments are already exhausting her, and she hasn't even gotten that many.

The second she said the word "*cancer,*" my knees gave out. I up and moved back immediately. Work was understanding, and I can do most of it from my phone anyway. It's just call after call, trying to help clients find leads for the jobs they have.

But it became the perfect reason to return. To face Alina after all this time. If Mom can face what she's going through again, then I can man up and finally talk to Alina while I'm in town.

The only thing is getting her to actually communicate with me.

Olivia plops the muffin and coffee down in front of me, pulling me from my thoughts. I was so lost, I almost forgot where I was.

"That'll be five seventy."

With a smile, I give her a ten. "Keep the change."

"I don't want your pity, Cameron."

"Consider it a tip for customer service with such a smiling face." I turn to leave, taking a big bite of my muffin. A moan pulls from my throat, and I swallow it down with a swig of delicious coffee. "Tell Alina I'll be back tomorrow." I talk through a mouthful of the most incredible muffin I've ever eaten and walk through the door and back to my car.

The problem with being back but having no job here and nobody to talk to is that there's nowhere else to go but home.

I could get some more work done, but I've been at it since seven this morning. Mom's usually resting, and I don't like to wake her.

Instead, I set off for a destination that only Alina would know where to find me.

Chapter 5
Alina

I don't understand how Cameron hasn't given up yet. It's been another two weeks, and he's *still* coming by daily.

After my little stunt with the muffin, he started asking some more specific questions. Like what my hours were, as though I have any.

"I can't keep running interference for you, Leen. At some point, you have to come out and say something to him. At least tell him to stop coming by."

"That's the problem, Liv. I don't know if I can. You *know* how much Cameron meant to me."

"Right. *Meant* to you."

I bite my lower lip as I turn to her, my fingers drumming on the counter.

"Wait, wait, wait. You can't possibly be trying to tell me that after all this time, you still have feelings for him. After everything he put you through."

That's the reminder I don't need. My heart shattered when he left without a trace. And it's never fully healed. But Cameron will always be somebody special to me. "He'll always be somebody of importance, Liv. He was my everything and went through so much with me. That doesn't just go away because he did."

"But it's been ten years. You were almost engaged to somebody else, for God's sake."

"And you know why I didn't allow that to happen." Come on, Liv. Put the pieces together.

"Because you didn't love Sean enough. But I never thought that meant that you still harbored feelings for Cameron." She says both names with disgust. She was never a fan of Sean; didn't think he was exciting enough. It's true he was a bit bland, in all things. But Cameron had been the one who was exciting. I thought I wanted the opposite of that.

"I don't know that I do. It's very confusing. Think about how you felt after Jay left."

She stiffens and straightens, fiddling with her massive engagement ring. I know she doesn't like to talk about that time.

"That was different. I chased him away and told him to leave."

"But he was still gone. And you still loved him, even though you thought you'd never see him again."

"He didn't just disappear one day, though. That's what Cameron did, Alina. Or need I remind you." Her tone is chastising.

"Trust me, I haven't forgotten. I can't explain what's going on inside me. It's scary. I don't know why he's here, why he's back, or why he's so adamant about talking to me. But I'm curious."

"Then maybe you need to face him."

"I'm scared." It comes out on a breath. The truest emotion rising to the surface.

Liv takes my hand in hers and squeezes so that my gaze focuses on her. "I know, LeeLee. But you have to jump. At least find out why he's here."

She's right, of course, but it's easier said than done.

"Today, I'm going to not be here when he comes in. Force you two to have it out."

My eyes widen and horror coils up my spine. "You're going to leave?"

She nods resolutely. "I am. You need to do this, Alina. I can't keep being this third party. And you didn't want Mazie to get involved, though she's offered several times."

Mazie would be almost as bad as Eli, who already threatened to march down here and plant himself in one of the booths for the day so he could "give Cameron a talking to." If I wasn't sure that conversation would end with fists being thrown, I'd maybe let him.

But Mazie would stand her ground and just insult him. I'd never learn why he's here or what he wants because Mazie would be too busy telling him all the things wrong with him, about his leaving, and that he has no right to be back. A speech I heard a bit too much of when Liv and I finally disclosed he was back.

Jameson thinks I should talk to him. Not that he knows the details of the sordid past, but I'm sure Liv said something. He just wasn't around to see the devastation left in Cameron's wake.

"What do I say?" I chew the inside of my lip as I think about talking to Cameron and having to collide with those brilliant blue-green eyes of his. They're almost turquoise in the right light, and they've always captivated me, made me unable to think. That's the biggest reason I can't talk to him. I'll lose my ability to form sentences and know what I'm doing and saying.

"Just wait on him like any other customer. Then you decide if you want to listen."

For being the youngest, Liv really is full of wisdom.

An hour and a half later, Liv is grabbing her jacket to leave. Fall has rolled in in full force with its crisp breeze and cool air.

"I'll be back in an hour or two. I'm going to go see Jay over at the hotel."

"Tell me again." There's a waver in my voice as I wonder if I can do this.

She grabs my shoulders and makes sure I'm facing her straight on. "You got this. You can do this."

Tight-lipped, I nod, and she pulls me in for a fierce hug.

Without a word, she grabs the coffee she made for Jameson. I'm incredibly envious of their relationship and how much they care for one another. He really crashed into her life and changed it for the better.

She's gone for all of fifteen minutes when the bell chimes and I nearly jump out of my skin. But it's not Cameron. It's just Mrs. Junish, here for her midday caffeine fix. We have quite a few regulars.

I help her with her order before resuming my pacing behind the counter, trying to take deep breaths every few minutes in an effort to calm my racing heart.

When the bell chimes again, it doesn't matter how much deep breathing I was doing because I forget to breathe altogether as all the air whooshes out of my lungs.

It's not fair that he looks so damn good after ten years. He's broad shouldered, muscles evident despite his light fall jacket, though clearly not bulky like Zachary. His height has always been something that wowed me as he'd tower over me. It seems his dirty blond hair has gotten darker as time has passed, but he still keeps it a bit longer on the top.

It's the second his eyes lock on mine that I'm done for.

Chapter 6

Cameron

I stop mid-step as I walk through the door to the café. Alina's not just out of her hiding spot behind that damn black door, but the only one here today. Liv is nowhere to be found, and unless she's traded places with Alina for today, she's not present.

Alina is just as captivating as ever. Her chocolate hair falls in long curls over her shoulders and those caramel eyes are soft and liquid as they glance at me.

With a quick shake of my head, I let the door close behind me and slowly make my way to the counter, hands shoved into my pockets.

Though I can tell she's bouncing on her toes, Alina stands tall.

"Hello. Can I help you?"

"Alina." Just saying her name again feels right in so many ways. Sure, I've been saying it for weeks, but not *to* her.

"Yes?" She won't focus on me, looking just past my shoulder.

"Look at me. Please." I need those beautiful eyes on mine. I need to see them.

"I can't do that, Cameron. Your eyes have always made me stupid, and I need to keep my faculties about me right now."

I stifle a laugh. It's something she used to tell me all the time. I'd use it to my advantage constantly to distract her. But I doubt that it will work right now.

"Okay. I can respect that."

"What can I get you?"

"Five minutes of your time. Please." Though her eyes move, they don't come any closer to landing on mine. Instead, they stay firmly on her hands, which are folded on the counter.

"I'm listening."

Now that I have her attention, or at least I'm pretty sure I do, I don't even know where to begin. There's so much to say, a decade's worth. How can I do that in five minutes?

"I'm sorry." It's the first thing that comes to mind and maybe the most important.

A sharp intake of breath tells me I'm on the right track. There's no doubt she hates me, but the fact that she's standing here at all is a good sign. One that makes me hopeful.

"I've never stopped thinking about you, Ali." She stiffens at my old nickname for her. I was the only one to shorten the beginning of her name. I needed to do something different, a way to stand out and for the name to be mine and mine alone.

"You have a funny way of showing it." The hurt lacing her words slices through me.

"I know. I'm sorry."

"What am I supposed to do with that? After ten years, you come back and apologize, and I'm supposed to...what?"

"Go on a date with me." The words fly out of my mouth faster than I can process them and take me by surprise.

But Alina's so stunned she literally takes a step backward, her hand flying to her mouth. Her eyes finally lock on mine and shock reverberates through her expression.

"Why would I do that?"

"I don't know. It just came out. But I mean it, Alina. Let me take you on a date. Let me try to explain myself."

"I—I..." She looks around frantically, like she's waiting for somebody to save her, but there's nobody here to intervene.

"Do you have any more of those chocolate caramel muffins?"

Her brows furrow, and she looks over at me again, this time calmer. "What?"

"Those chocolate caramel muffins you had the other day, they were amazing. Definitely my new favorite. Do you happen to have any more?" I'm hoping I can distract her from the blurting of my date proposal by getting onto another topic.

The slightest of smiles graces her face before she turns back to me, all business. "Sorry, we don't have any today. But we do have pumpkin, banana nut, corn, and blueberry."

"The pumpkin sounds delicious. Very seasonal. I'll take one of those and just a large black coffee, please."

The way her shoulders relax makes me think she's grateful to have a task at hand instead of having to maintain small talk. And she sets about her mission dutifully, grabbing the muffin from the case and placing it in a bag.

"I'd like to eat here today. I won't request that you sit with me, but I'm going to sit over at one of those tables, by myself, to eat. If that's okay with you." I point in the general direction of whatever random table I'll grab to eat at.

"Of course. We don't turn away patrons. All are welcome to stay and eat." The smile on her face looks forced now, and while I'm sure it's uncomfortable for her, I need to be in her presence longer. Liv can chase me out if she comes back.

Taking my muffin and coffee, I nod and walk over to a table, plopping myself in the chair that only half faces the counter. I want Alina to know I'm here but don't want her to feel like I'm just going to sit here and watch her.

Instead, I focus on the food in front of me. It's delicious, of course. Everything Alina makes is.

It's not until I'm on the last bite that I feel a presence behind me. I'd become so focused on my food that I lost track of Alina. I turn around and look up. She's standing there with her hands clasped in front of her apron, looking around the café instead of at me.

"Yes."

My brows furrow, and I sling my arm over the back of the chair. "I'm sorry?"

"Yes. I'll go on a date with you."

My eyes widen, and I jump to stand. It feels impolite to remain seated.

"Really?" Shock courses through me, my heartbeat rocketing in my chest.

"Yes."

"Okay then. Friday. I'll pick you up here at seven?"

"That sounds fine." Not necessarily the reaction I was hoping for, but I'll take it. A tentative smile pulls up the corners of my mouth. Not enough to potentially scare her off, but existent all the same.

"I'll see you then."

She takes my words as a dismissal and walks straight back into the kitchen.

I clean my mess up and head out to my car with a little more pep in my step.

Today is a good day.

Chapter 7
Alina

"Why did I agree to go on a date with him? What the hell was I thinking?"

"I have no fucking idea. What *were* you thinking?" Mazie watches me as I stalk past her chair again. I called in reinforcements today because I'm sure I've lost my damn mind.

"It's those damn eyes. I'm a damn sucker for those eyes." Their aquamarine caught me off guard just as much as I feared they would.

"I'll gouge them out for you. Sound good?" She seems a little too excited about the prospect.

I pause my trek around the office and plant my hands firmly on my hips. "I know you want his head on a platter, Mazie, but come on now. He apologized."

"A blanket apology is not enough. What is he sorry for?"

"Maybe that's what the date is for. To tell me."

"You don't even know why he's back. What if he's engaged?"

Something akin to jealousy wraps around my heart and squeezes. Why would I be jealous? I hold no claim to him anymore.

"Then it's a final dinner between us before we officially part ways forever." I kneel down next to my sister and take her hand. "Mazie, I need you on my team. I'm nervous. But I need this as much as he does, and I didn't realize it until he brought it up. It's a chance for closure. Real closure I've never gotten with him."

"And what if all he wants is to get in your pants?" There's a possible reality to this statement that I hadn't considered before.

"First of all, he's never been like that. Second of all, I'm a grown woman and can tell him no."

"You couldn't say no to the date." She has a point there.

"Because I didn't want to. Saying no to dinner and letting him be with me again are two very different things."

"Maybe to you. What if they're not to him?"

"Then he'll learn the hard way that they are. But he's not like that." I'm making grand assumptions about somebody I used to know.

"You don't know what he's like Alina. It's been ten damn years. You're both different people now."

"I'm not so different, Maze." My fingers lock in front of me, and I look down at them as they intertwine. I'm still the girl who loves to bake and has nightmares more often than not.

"You may not see it, but I do." Sincerity sweeps through her tone. Of course Mazie sees a difference; she's watched me grow and helped me in that process. But I'm not that different from the girl I was when Cameron left. At least I don't feel it.

Maybe that's what this draw to him is. That I feel like the same person I was. And on some level, I must be hoping that he is too.

It's that moment that Liv returns, storming through the doors. "What the fuck did you do, Alina?"

I may have texted her an emergency 911 and to come back immediately. But Jameson's at least twenty minutes away so it took her a bit to get here.

While I'm too sheepish to answer, Mazie leans around me and answers for me. "She agreed to go on a date with him."

Liv's eyebrows reach her hairline, and her eyes widen so big, I'm afraid they may fall out of her skull. "You did *what?*"

"Agreed to go on a date. Just one." I barely mumble the words.

"You were supposed to get him coffee and a muffin and send him on his merry way. Listen to the five minutes of bullshit he had to spew and then tell him to leave." Liv's rambling angrily, and then she takes a look at me seated on the couch in Mazie's office, coming to sit next to me and taking my hands in hers. "What happened?"

"I don't really know. I was telling Mazie it's the eyes..."

"They make you stupid," Liv fills in for me.

"Yeah. And he asked me on a date, and I said yes. I don't know why. I think part of me is looking for closure and is hoping I'll get it. It felt wrong, Liv. To make him say it there. What if somebody came in?" I'm shaking my head as I talk, tears welling in my eyes. "I need to know what he has to say and why he left. And I need to do it on my terms, which isn't standing behind the counter at the café, unable to look at him."

"I can understand that. We're just worried about you, LeeLee." Liv's tone has softened, and I know she's holding in strong emotions for me.

Everybody used to love Cameron. Then he left, and my pain turned into their hatred. But even I haven't ever been able to bring myself to that level.

The amount of love I had for him prevented that, no matter how deeply the wounds went. And boy were they deep.

Over time, it dwindled away, but it never turned to hatred.

"I know you guys are worried, but don't be. Cameron can't possibly hurt me more than he already has. And all this can do is help. Help me heal and find closure." Maybe the wounds will finally scar instead of remaining scabbed over.

"I guess you have a point there. Just be careful." Mazie's motherly tone has taken over, and I know we've lost our sister. She's in mom mode now.

"It's the only way I know how to be." Cameron's leaving instilled that caution in me. I've had walls miles high built around myself since he left. Not even Sean was able to break them down much. But I let him in more than any other man because he felt safe, the very opposite of Cameron in many ways.

Where Cameron was athletic, a star football player, Sean was more of a chess club kind of guy. Where Cameron had been—and still looks—built and muscular, Sean was long and lean. They were mostly polar opposites in every way. But I never truly loved Sean, much to his dismay.

"When is the date?" Liv's voice pulls me from my reverie.

"Friday."

"So, we have three days to prepare you for this."

"*Prepare* feels like a strong word. It's just a date."

"With your first love who I'm kind of certain you never got over but have been so hurt by you can't see that."

Liv's words shock me into stillness.

"I mean, come on, Alina. Sean may have been boring, but he treated you like a damn princess. And you couldn't love him. You barely even let him know you, and after two years and an almost proposal, wouldn't even live with him. You barely spent the night together!" Sometimes I hate that my sister is my best friend and I confide all these things in her.

"So, you think I'm still in love with him?"

Both of them sigh heavily, and I don't miss the look they share. But I remain silent, waiting for one of them to answer me.

"It's not that we think you're still in love with him, per se. It's more that we think you never really closed that chapter and we're worried you'll let him back in."

I stand quickly, indignation rising within me. "Isn't that my choice? Yes, he hurt me, but isn't it my choice if I want to let him back in? Which, I'm not even sure why we're talking about that because it's just a date and he may be getting married for all we know. But it's my life and my choice as to whether I let him in again or not. Right?"

"We just don't want to see you hurt, Alina. That was hard on all of us. And I swear this time I may not be able to stop Eli from killing him." Mazie shivers at the thought. Eli was ready to track him down and beat him lifeless for how upset I was.

I was never really sure what happened there except that nobody knew where Cameron had run off to, so nobody knew how to find him. His parents, who I thought had adored me, shut me out and never said a word. They don't even come by the café much. It's like they never got over it either.

With a shake of my head, I get rid of all the negativity. "This is going to be good, guys. And I need you on my side, so I need you believing it will be too. At the very least to give me some closure."

They exchange another quick glance, and then their gazes lock on me before they smile. It's almost eerie how in sync they are. "You got it, Leen. We're always on your side, but if you want us to be positive, we will be."

"Good. That's what I need right now."

"Then that's what you'll have." Liv squeezes my hand and smiles.

Positivity. I need it from them because while I'm putting on a brave front, I'm absolutely panicking. My insides are a jumbled mess, and I can barely catch my breath. They need to be able to help ground me and keep me levelheaded while I go into this date.

Because I worry that Liv might be right, and I never really let Cameron go.

Chapter 8

Cameron

I still can't believe Alina agreed to the date. I've been into the café every day since, as has she, and every day I've expected her to cancel.

Instead, she's been cordial and waits on me. The change is mind boggling.

But Friday is here, and I'm bouncing on the balls of my feet about an hour before I have to pick her up. I've already had to change my shirt twice from sweating through it. I'm that damn nervous.

I don't know what to expect from this. It was my offer, but it came from a place of desperation. Not that I don't want to go out with Alina, but I have no idea what to say or talk about. It's been a damn decade.

I've never stopped loving her. This I know for certain. I've made peace with the fact that I'll likely never be with her again, and this date doesn't change that, because for all I know, she has a serious boyfriend. There's no ring on her finger, but she's a baker and chef. Maybe she takes it off during the day so she doesn't get it messy.

What if she is engaged? This might just be closure for her, an official goodbye since I never gave her one to begin with.

Dammit. I'm starting to get sweaty again.

Deep breaths.

I can't just stand here in my childhood bedroom and wait for the time I need to leave, so I go check on Mom.

She's been sleeping for most of the day, but when I get to her room, she's sitting up and watching TV. She looks so different from the mom I've always known. Smaller and more frail. But that megawatt smile graces her face as I walk in regardless.

"Well, you look handsome. Going somewhere?"

"I have a date, actually."

"A date? Anybody I know?"

I clear my throat. "Alina."

Her mouth opens and then closes before opening again. "Alina Baker, Alina?"

"Are there any others in Juniper Grove?" Alina's not exactly a popular name.

I push off the doorframe where I've been leaning and walk to sit on the edge of her bed.

"I just haven't heard that name in a while is all. It took me by surprise. So that's where you've been going every day? To her café?" Mom's always been perceptive.

"Yes." I've mostly stayed in the house, taking care of Mom, the house, or working while Dad's at work himself. But every day, at the same time, I leave to go to the café.

"You know it's been a while since I've been there. Dad's gone a few times since, I think. But not me. It was always tough to be near her and I tried to stay quiet, afraid I might divulge something I shouldn't. She was always such a lovely girl."

"I've never stopped loving her, Mom. Never. Even after all these years. And I know it's possible she's moved on or wants nothing to do with me based on how I left things, but I have to try." It's been ages since I've had this heartfelt of a conversation with my mother, but somehow, I think the prospect of her dying has changed things tremendously.

"I think I've always known that."

"How?" I lift my gaze to meet hers. Even the sparkle that used to reside in her blue eyes when she looked at me is gone.

"I'm your mother, for one. We have ways of knowing things. But you always asked about her. Even after it had been a year, then five years, even just before you came home. You always asked how Alina was doing or the café or the Bakers in general. You wouldn't do that if you stopped caring about her." The softness in her tone reminds of being a child with a skinned knee.

"Am I crazy for not letting go? It's been a long time."

"It certainly has been, but no. Alina was somebody very important to you. It makes sense you still hold some sort of flame for her."

"It feels like more than that, Mom. When I saw her again...it was like no time had passed and all those feelings rushed back. I could smell the flour and sugar on her." The corners of my lips pull up as I remember. God, I can't wait to see this woman.

"Just be careful, Cameron. I try not to listen to too much gossip about the Bakers with our history being what it is, but she's had a rough go of things." It makes my heart skip as I think about what she possibly could have been through aside from the loss of her parents.

"I will be. For all I know, she just wants this to be a closure thing. Which I'm okay with if that's what she needs." The thought has been plaguing my mind, and if that's all Alina wants out of tonight, then I'll find a way to be okay with it. Because I'm hoping this is my way back into her life. That I can talk to her and show her that I'm more than my past.

That's what my life has been about since then. Moving on from my past and being a better person.

The biggest concern I have is that I'll have to tell Alina what pulled me away from her in the first place. She'll look at me differently after that. Especially because I was struggling and didn't let her know.

I'll be lucky if she ever trusts me again.

"Shit, I gotta go. I can't be even a second late."

"Language."

"Mom. Really?" I tilt my head to the side and look at her with a raised eyebrow. I'm twenty-eight, for fuck's sake.

"Yes. I'm still your mother. Honor my dying wishes." A chill creeps up my spine and works its way through my extremities.

"Don't talk like that."

She takes my hand and pats it gently. "I'm sorry. Just trying to be realistic."

It may be the reason I came home, but it's something I'm unwilling to face.

"Well, you're not dying tonight, so I get to say *shit*. I'll be home later. Hopefully not too soon, though."

"No funny business, mister. This is the first time you're seeing this girl in a decade."

"Ew, Mom, no. I just meant that I hope it goes well and she doesn't turn me away too soon. That we get to enjoy a nice dinner and maybe some dessert. Nothing sexual."

"Alright. Now you run along. Tell Alina I said hello and that I hope she's well."

"I will."

With a quick kiss on her forehead, I leave her to her shows. I know she likes to catch up on the drama she misses during the week when she's too tired to watch. I swing through the garage and tell Dad I'm leaving so he knows he's on Mom duty. He's taken to fiddling with random shit while Mom goes through her treatments. Something about his anxiety and stress.

I get to the café five minutes early and look through my windshield and the front window. There're a few people milling about, blocking my view of the counter to see if Alina's in there.

With a deep breath, I get out of the car and go inside. I barely hear the bell chime above my head because in that instant, the crowd seems to part like the red sea, and I get a full-on glimpse of Alina.

Her dark curls are flowing around her shoulders, full and shiny. She's wearing a pair of dark-wash jeans and a light blue shirt that's tight across her midsection but flowy in the arms. But the most breathtaking part is her smile. Her head is thrown back while she laughs, a hand resting on her chest and all her teeth are on display as she makes the musical sound.

I'm utterly frozen in place by her. My breath is stolen.

But as I get closer, she notices me and stops laughing. Her cheeks redden, and she clears her throat, almost like she's embarrassed she was having a good time before I got here.

"Alina."

"Cameron."

"Are you ready?" Liv and Mazie are both here, and both have their arms crossed as they shoot daggers at me.

"Just a sec." Alina disappears behind the black door, but reappears just as quickly, sliding a small black purse onto her shoulder.

She rests a hand on both her sisters' arms as they come to a huddle.

Hushed voices mumble but nothing is discernible. From the looks of it, Alina's telling them to calm down, because they both glance over at me and their gazes soften.

They have an awkward three-way hug before Alina turns to me, this time with a smile all for me. "Okay. I'm ready."

I extend an elbow for her to take. It's a risky move, and I know it as soon as she eyes my arm and glances up at my face and then back down at my arm again. But I'm trying to be a gentleman and that states that I give her my arm.

Cautiously, she takes it, and every nerve in my body jumps to attention. It's been ten years since Alina has touched me, and it's like I've waited every single day for this to happen again.

A sigh eases from my lips as I lead her toward the door.

"Not too late, you two." The sternness in Mazie's voice rings out behind us, and I fight the urge to roll my eyes. Ever the mother, rarely the sister.

Besides the tiny "thank you" I get for holding the door to the café and car open for her, the first several minutes of our date are silent. I have no idea how to break the ice and cut through the very thick tension that's wrapped around us.

When we get onto the highway, Alina pipes up. "Where are we going?"

"I wanted to take you to Rosalind's."

She glances down at her outfit, then over at mine. She may just now be noticing that I'm wearing dress pants and a sport coat over my button-down. Sans tie, though.

"I'm not dressed for Rosalind's." Panic creeps into her voice.

"Nonsense. You look beautiful." I glance between her and the road a few times before focusing back on what lies ahead of me.

The rest of the twenty-minute drive is surrounded by nothing besides the songs on the radio, which is at a low hum.

Something's going to have to give, or this is going to be the worst date in history.

Chapter 9
Alina

I was hoping the awkwardness would dissipate as we got to Rosalind's. It hasn't. Now the only saving grace is that we have our menus to occupy our attention. Not that I need mine. I always get the same thing when I come here.

Though it's been ages since I've actually been to Rosalind's.

I know why Cameron chose it. And it's not just because it's one of the nicest restaurants within a thirty-minute radius. It's because this is where he first told me he loved me. On some level, he wants me to remember the good parts of our relationship.

What he doesn't realize is that I've never forgotten. Many of them have just been overshadowed by his disappearance.

While it's something I want to tell him, I don't exactly know how to bring it up. Not to mention, he was thoughtful enough to make a reservation for tonight. It tells me he put thought and care into this date, and it wasn't just on a whim.

I hear him flip closed his menu, but I hide farther behind mine, lowering my head a touch. A chuckle rings through my ears.

"I don't honestly believe you're not getting the chicken Milanese. It's always been your favorite."

My shoulders push back, and I raise my chin, closing my menu and setting it in front of me. "A lot can change in a decade, Cameron."

"I miss you calling me Cam." There's sadness lacing his words and passing through his eyes.

"Well, I don't know you anymore. You're a different person now."

"I'm not so different." Isn't this the same argument I had with Mazie earlier, only about myself? Now Cameron's throwing it back at me.

"We don't know each other anymore. It's been ten years and a lot can change in ten years. Even if we're still similar to the people we were before, there's a lot of time for things to have happened that changed us." I readjust the napkin on my lap. The dim lighting makes the sadness in his eyes all the more painful.

"I want to know you again, Alina. It's part of why I'm back."

"Why'd you leave?" The words slip from my mouth fast and with desperation. But really, it's the only question I want an answer to. Nothing else matters. Because for years I've been blaming myself.

"I...I want to tell you. Trust me, I do. But here and now is not the time." His tone has changed and there's a finality to it, but also sincerity. Others wouldn't be able to pick up on the subtleties in the way he speaks, but I knew him so well at one point.

"Why did you seek me out this time? I know you can't possibly have never come back before. Why now?"

"Some things are...changing. Again, a conversation for another time. But I've never stopped thinking about you, Alina. I've never stopped missing you. It just never felt right before. It never felt like a good time. And I'm not sure this is either. But I got tired of waiting. I learned more of the frailty of life, and it gave me a reason to just jump."

The frailty of life? Has he lost somebody? Maybe he was married, and his wife died, and now he's back to rekindle with me. That doesn't make sense, but something certainly happened to him.

"What does that mean? What are you hoping for in all of this? I came here assuming you wanted closure. To explain what happened and tie things up with a neat little bow. But you seemed to have planned those conversations for a later time."

"I want to be part of your life again."

All the air whooshes from my body and the blood pools at my feet.

Can I let him in again? The thing is, I want to. Because after all this time, sitting here with him now, feels right in a way nothing has in ten years.

"You're going to have to work for it, Cameron."

"I'm absolutely willing to go through any trials you throw my way, Alina. You're worth it." His fingers flutter against the table, and I can tell he's thinking of taking my hand but opts not to.

"How do you know that? What if I'm not anymore."

"Impossible." Our gazes lock, and it's like I'm completely stuck in this moment with Cameron.

It's that second the waiter chooses to come over. "What can I get for you this evening?"

Cameron doesn't take his eyes off me as I order my chicken Milanese, bringing a smile to his face. Nor does he take them off me as he orders the veal parmigiana.

When the waiter departs with a bow, Cameron extends his hand, palm up. "Please, Alina. Say you'll let me try to get in your good graces again. I know I don't deserve it, and I'll spend every day showing you how much I appreciate the ability to try."

I hesitate, not really sure what to think or do or feel in this moment. But it's Cameron. And I realize with a sense of unsettledness, that Liv was right, I never truly got over him. And he's sitting here, across from me, wanting to hold my hand and pleading to let him try to make things right between us. How do I say no to that?

I don't.

So instead, I place my hand in his and nod. "Okay, Cameron. I'll let you try. But you're going to have to be open and honest with me."

He wraps his fingers around mine and squeezes. "I will. I promise. I have nothing to hide, Alina. I want you to know the truth. This just isn't the place for it." His brows furrow as he looks around.

"You didn't have to bring me here to remind me of the good times, Cameron. I remember."

"I know there are more bad than good, though. I wanted to bring you here and have you remember some of the best ones. Like after prom. And when I told you I loved you." His eyes sparkle with longing I recognize.

"I've never forgotten. And some things may be overshadowed by the bad, but it's all here." I point to my head. "It's just become a bit more gray instead of black and white."

It used to be easy to tell the good times from the bad with Cameron. The happy times from the fights, the hard times, the sad times. He broke his wrist his junior year of high school, effectively ending his football career, even though he was being scouted for college. That was a very hard time, but we leaned on each other, and I thought we were going to come out ahead.

Until he disappeared about a year later. That's when everything became murky. I couldn't tell if the good times were actually good or just a charade we were carrying on. Or maybe I was good, and he wasn't, and I didn't know. What had happened between us to make him leave without a word?

It's something I've wondered for a decade.

I pull my hand from his as the ache starts in my chest. The same one that always happens when I think about him leaving and what it meant.

"Tell me what to do, Alina. Tell me what to do and I'll do it. Anything."

"I want to know why you left."

"And I promise I'll tell you. Soon."

Our food arrives before I can ask any other questions. The rest of dinner goes by in a bit of a haze, as I wonder what he's thinking, how he's feeling, what he did in all his time away. Surely, he had girlfriends. Did he ever come close to proposing to one? Or could he not get to that point with anybody else like I couldn't with Sean?

There are so many thoughts and questions and feelings whirling through my body, I barely eat. It's like I've lost my appetite. Cameron notices and stops eating too, asking for the check so we can leave.

The only sound on the way home is the din from the radio. I can't even tell what station he has it on but if things are still the same, it's the local rock station.

When we get to my house from my very limited directions, he doesn't hesitate to get out of the car and run around to my side, opening the door for me and extending a hand to help me out.

He shoves his hands in his pockets as we walk to the front door.

"I'm sorry if this was awkward, Alina. I just want another chance. That's all."

"I know. There's just a lot going on with that."

He sighs and runs a hand through his dirty blond hair. "I'm sure there is. And it's my fault. But I meant it when I said I'd make it up to you. I'll tell you what you want to know, and I'll make everything right again. I just need time. Can you give me that?"

I raise my eyes to look at him, finding brows furrowing. He's hopeful. "I can. But know you'll have to go through Liv and Mazie too. I don't even know about Eli." A chill travels through me at the thought of them running into each other again.

"I told you, I'm willing to face anything you throw my way. That includes your siblings. They're part of you, Alina. I'm here for all of it. Every second." He makes a slight movement, like he wants to reach out and take my hands but then they drop back to his sides.

With a deep breath, I put my fingers on his forearm, which causes his shoulders to lower. "Good. I'm glad."

"I'll be by the café again tomorrow. I'm not stopping just because you agreed to a date with me."

"I'll see you then."

With a tight-lipped nod, he squeezes my hand and retreats off the steps.

I let myself into the house and fall against the door. Dinner was awkward as hell, and I didn't get any of the answers I was looking for. But Cameron wants to try again. And I'd be a damn liar if I said part of me wasn't hoping that's what he wanted all along.

Now I just have to tell my sisters.

Chapter 10

Cameron

I've been trying for two days not to kick myself for dinner. I feel like I should have planned better, thought out what to talk about beforehand, something. But instead, I floundered. And let Alina flounder with me.

The past few days in the café have been about as awkward as our date. Now that we've talked more, it just feels like there's something else in the air. But each day she's waited on me, getting me my muffin and coffee, albeit while Liv watched from close by. That's new.

But expected. She's a touch more cordial than she had been. Only a touch. There's not as much disdain in her voice when she greets me.

Day three after our date, something has to give.

"Good afternoon, ladies."

"Hello, Cameron." There's no disdain, but Liv's tone isn't pleasant either. I can tell she doesn't trust me still. All in good time.

"What can I get you today?" Alina at least greets me with a slight smile.

"Hmm." I browse the baked goods case and find the chocolate caramel muffins are back. "I think you can probably guess." I take my chances and shoot her a wink.

Her cheeks pinken in the cutest way. I've always loved making Alina blush. Something about it makes her look so incredibly sweet and angelic.

She bends down and pulls out one of the chocolate muffins while Liv gets my coffee. "Large regular, right?"

"Yes, please," I answer Liv, but I can't tear my gaze from Alina. Something about her look today makes her absolutely stunning. Maybe it's the new pink tinge to her cheeks or the puff of flour she surely has no idea is in her hair. Maybe it's the lighting. I have no idea, but she's breathtaking.

When Alina puts up my muffin, I reach for it quickly so our fingers can brush, and electricity buzzes beneath my skin.

Her eyes dart up to meet mine.

"Will you sit with me today?" It's an impromptu question, but one I find I want to be asking all the same.

"Um." She's completely caught off guard. Her body has utterly frozen in place, and her eyebrows sit high on her forehead. Instead of answering me, she turns to Liv for approval, and I do too.

But Liv just shrugs. She knows that this isn't her choice to make and that Alina needs to start doing these things herself.

As she turns back to me, that pink hue still resides in her cheeks. "Sure. I'll sit with you. Let me just make a quick coffee."

I settle at the table that's become mine, the one I randomly picked a few days ago. The bell chimes as a group of people comes in, and I can't help but think it's perfect timing because it will help distract Liv from the fact that Alina and I are sitting together.

Alina takes a seat across from me just as I take a large bite of muffin. I freeze and look at her, but she has a hand over her mouth as she stifles a laugh.

"These are really delicious, by the way," I say through a mouthful of food.

"I had a feeling you'd like them. Still a sucker for caramel, I see."

"Always." There's a reason for that, and not just because it's delicious, but it's something to share another day.

"Good to know some things don't change."

The smile falls from my face. "A lot of things haven't, Alina." I reach out and take her hand. Her breath catches, and she looks down at where we're connected.

"I guess so." Something about the way she says it makes me think she's not talking about my love of caramel anymore.

"So tell me, what do you do besides work here?"

She stares at me blankly and blinks a few times.

"Ah, so nothing. Really? You don't do anything for fun?" She was always more of a homebody.

"Every so often, Liv and I will go dancing. But that's much less now that she's with Jameson."

"Yes, Jameson. Seems like a nice guy. I'm surprised I don't see him around here more often since I'm here every day. He's Liv's fiancé, right?" I take another bite, quickly followed by a sip of coffee.

"Husband, actually." She holds her cup between both hands and looks down into the dark liquid. I can't tell if she's upset that Liv got married first. That never seemed to matter to her. "He's working out by Pineville City, so he doesn't come in as much right now. She goes to him more often. But when he's not working, he's here every day."

"And do you approve of him for Liv?"

Now a smile widens across her face, and she nods as she sinks into her chair. "I do. He's great for her. Got a lot of money, which doesn't matter, but he's from Manhattan so he can give her that city life she's always wanted. Or at least a taste of it. They kept his apartment down there so they can go for the weekend whenever they want to."

Liv's big dreams of the city. She's been talking about leaving this tiny town and getting down there for as long as I can remember.

"That sounds like the perfect solution for her. So, they're living here full time then?"

"Yeah, they're actually house hunting right now. Jameson wants something a little bigger. He spoils the crap out of Liv. Have you seen her ring? I mean, my God, I don't even know how she holds her damn hand up half the time." She giggles, and it lights me up. It feels so carefree to be here like this.

"I've seen it. Pretty big."

"A little ostentatious, in my opinion, but that's Jameson. He's big on giving Liv everything she'd ever want in life and going grand with it. I'm sure they'll buy the biggest house they can find in Juniper Grove." She rolls her eyes but giggles again while she does it before taking a sip of her coffee. "How about you? Are you working while you're visiting?"

"I am. I can do ninety-nine percent of my job from my phone or computer. The rest, I have somebody else helping with."

"What do you do exactly?"

I take a sip of coffee to help swallow down the bite of muffin I took. "I help companies find employees. Not quite a headhunter but similar. A company will call me and tell me what they're looking for, and I help them find people through our list of employees who are looking for jobs."

"Oh, that sounds..."

"Boring. It's incredibly boring. But it pays well."

She leans to the side as she laughs. "I guess that's the most you can ask for."

"I was happy to hear you guys had opened the café. It seems perfect for your talents. And the food is certainly as delicious as I remember your cooking to be." To enforce that thought, I take another large bite of my muffin, a light 'mmm' escaping. It's truly delicious. And sadly, almost gone.

"It seemed the most fitting thing to do with what everybody wanted. Liv's less than thrilled being out front, but I help her a lot, and we have a small staff. They're here more now that she takes a little more time out of town."

I glance around at the establishment, taking in the cutesy signs, the wall of mugs, and the handwritten menu. Clearly Mazie's handwriting, as she always had that artsy flare. "It's a great environment. I'm proud of you."

While I want to ask about the rest of her siblings and see how they're doing, to bring up the fact that her parents always wanted to open *something,* and I think honoring them with a café is a great idea, I don't know how she handles talking about that these days. I'm still new at this, and I don't want to fuck anything up yet. I'm surely bound to, but hopefully it's later on when we're more established and she's more inclined to forgive me.

"Thank you."

"I'd love to see your workspace someday."

"Oh, we don't let too many people back there. Even Jameson just started being allowed back in the past few months and he and Liv have been together for over a year now." Her perfectly plump lower lip lands between her teeth as she slouches forward.

"That's okay. At some point, I'd like to see it. I want to know about you, Alina. And I know that this café and the things you make for it are a huge part of your life and your day-to-day. So I'd like to see your safe space and where the magic happens."

"That's sweet of you, but I'm not sure it's magic."

"Are you kidding me? This is the best muffin I've ever tasted. And all the others are right up there." I'm not sure if Alina's just being humble or if she really doesn't think that her baked goods are as above par as they are.

"You're really being too kind. But I do love being able to bake every day."

"I'm glad you're putting your talents to good use."

A silence takes over as neither of us seems to know what to say without small talk. There are so many deeper conversations to be having, but now isn't the time or place.

"Can I see you outside of here again? Maybe something a little more personal next time?"

"Are you inviting yourself over?" One of her eyebrows cocks high on her forehead.

"Of course not. I'd never do such a thing. But I'm staying with my folks so there's no real privacy there, and I'd just like to see you outside of work and awkward dinners. Somewhere we can talk. There's a lot to be said and heard."

She chews the inside of her lip as she looks toward her sister, surely wondering what she'd have to say about the situation. But it's not Liv's decision to make and Alina must realize that because she turns to me and straightens.

"How about tonight? Come by around six? I'll make dinner."

"You don't have to do that."

"I know. But I'd like to. I have to eat anyway, may as well make something for both of us." She shrugs a shoulder like it's no big deal. She's going to cook for me. It's been ages since she's done that. I don't count the muffins, that's baking. Alina's a different chef when she cooks.

"That sounds amazing. I'll be there, six o'clock on the dot."

"Good. I'm going to get back to it now. I have to replenish the scones; they were big sellers today, and we tend to get a rush around the end of the school day." Her chair scrapes against the floor as she pushes it back to stand.

"Of course. Don't let me keep you. Thanks for sitting with me today."

"I was happy to, Cameron. I'm giving this a shot because I want to also. It's not just one-sided." She pauses next to my chair and rests her hand on my shoulder. All the air sticks in my lungs, and it's almost like I've forgotten how to breathe.

"I'll see you tonight."

She gives me a curt nod and walks behind the counter, brushing her hand over Liv's shoulders as she continues through the black door.

Tonight. It's the only thing that's going to keep me going today, knowing that I get to see Alina again in a much more intimate setting.

We can finally talk and share the bigger things. Things I want her to know.

While the thought is somewhat exhilarating, it's also terrifying. Because now, I have to be open and honest with her. What if she never looks at me the same way again?

Chapter 11
Alina

Cameron showed up at six exactly. Not a minute before, not a minute after. I'm happy he was on time because I was practically bouncing out of my skin with anticipation.

But dinner has been nice. We discussed business some more, and he seems really interested in the café. He asked after Mazie and Eli. It was an easy conversation to have with him, though I expected a repeat of the other night. I think the more personal and quiet setting helped. There was less pressure somehow.

And I'm in the comfort of my home. It's easy to relax when I'm in my space.

He was impressed with the modest house as he walked in. It's nothing too extravagant, a single floor home with a stunning kitchen, which is, of course, my favorite room of the house. I gave him a brief tour, and he had nothing but great things to say.

Part of me feels like he's being overly kind and generous, but he's never really been somebody to lie about things of that nature. He wouldn't compliment the house if he didn't really feel it was worth complimenting; he'd just sweep right past it.

I've kept things calm while we eat, but there are questions that are dying to burst out of me, ones I need answers to, especially if this...friendship is going to continue.

That's why when we finish eating, I'm happy he suggests sitting on the couch with our wine.

I curl my feet up to the side of me and lean against the arm of the couch while he sits on the other end. I give my glass a quick swirl as silence blankets us. It's less uncomfortable than the other night, though.

"Why did you leave, Cameron? What happened? What did I do that was so terrible you had to leave me?" The words leave my lips without restraint, and I almost cringe, but instead thank the liquid courage I've gained from the wine.

But Cameron does cringe. He looks at the ground and shakes his head. He had to know this was coming, but possibly not so bluntly. "It was never about you, Ali. It was me. I was going through...things. My own shit. I couldn't be around anymore. It wasn't good for me."

"I wasn't good for you?" My brows pull together as his words stab their way through my heart.

"No, baby." It's practically a whisper.

My heart seizes at him calling me *baby*. Like it's just so easy for him. And on some level, I think it is, because it's far easier than it should be for me to hear.

"No, never you. You were the best part of my life." Taking a deep breath, he scoots closer to me and runs his hand up my leg, squeezing my thigh as he looks down at where his hand rests. "I had an addiction, Alina. To pain pills."

My jaw drops, and along with it, my heart. "What?"

"Remember my injury? Junior year? They gave me really strong medicine for it because the break was pretty bad. And I became addicted. I couldn't get enough of the high, the numbness, the blankness it gave me. There was a guy in the class above us who sold...everything, really. I started buying from him first, then when he left, he hooked me up with somebody else."

My stomach clenches with unease. There's so much defeat in his voice, and he hasn't lifted his gaze, but all I want is to look into his eyes.

"I didn't know. How didn't I know? I was closest to you; we were together all the time. Literally every waking hour, and many non-waking, were spent together. How could I not have known?" The tears that had flooded my eyes in seconds fall over my lids and spill down my cheeks, thumping against my jeans.

Cupping my face, thumbs grazing along my cheekbones, he tilts up so that our eyes finally lock. Sadness and pain shroud his and my chest tightens at the sight. "Because I didn't want you to, Alina. I wanted to keep you from it. Hell, I kept everybody from it, but especially you. I knew it would hurt you, and I couldn't do that."

Because of my parents and how they died. He was addicted to getting high and my parents were murdered by somebody while high. He knew the effect that likely would have had on me. Or at least he thinks. Maybe then it would have bothered me more than it does now because it was raw and fresh. Or maybe now it doesn't affect me as much because it's *Cam*.

"One night, I reached a low. We had fought about something, my time and that you felt I was distant, which I was because I was thinking about getting away to go replace my stash. I went to my dad that night and told him about everything. I was gone a few days later."

Cameron swallows roughly as he looks away, sliding one hand to cup the back of my neck while the other moves to rest over my heart.

"Alina, I never meant to be away so long. My parents got me into a rehab near college. Then classes started and I was doing better, feeling better. Except I missed you horribly. The one time I came home, I nearly relapsed. Two years after I'd left, and all because of the pain of missing you. I came back to see my folks and saw you on the arm of another guy. Rumblings around town were that you two were likely to get engaged. That damn near killed me."

Sean. He'd heard about Sean. He'd heard about my probable engagement, meanwhile I'd never even known he was in Juniper Grove.

"You came back?" Some part of me always knew he had to be at least popping in now and then. But to hear him confirm it makes it different, too real.

"Of course I did. Many times."

"I never saw you, never knew." There's a desperation to my voice that I don't recognize. Would things have been any different if I'd known? Unlikely. But part of me feels like I missed out on something important.

"I made sure to stay quiet, as out of sight as possible. Mostly because I had been so certain you did in fact get engaged to whoever that guy was. I wouldn't have been able to stand that." His hand lowers from my chest to hold mine where it resides in my lap. I want it back on my chest, back to my heart.

"Did you not date for ten years?"

"Date? Sure. I had a casual girlfriend here or there. But never anything serious. Never anything that would be a long-term commitment. I couldn't. I wasn't in that place in life, that headspace. And none of them were you, nobody could ever be you, Alina."

My heart thumps erratically at his declaration.

"I've been clean for ten years. And for ten years, I've missed you every single day. I've wondered how different life could be now had I only just opened up to you then, told you what was going on. But I was so ashamed of myself. How could you love me still after being so weak? After giving in to such temptation?" There's a waver in his voice and a glassiness to his eyes. His hand grips the back of my neck harder as he pulls me inches closer.

It can't be easy for him to share this inner turmoil, these demons that he had to battle and is now having to face the consequences of. And the fact that he's had to do it all alone makes my heart heavy. Though I wish he would have confided me, pride swells in my chest that he's overcome so much.

"I wasn't good enough for you then, Alina. Hell, I'm not even good enough for you now. But I need you to see that so you can start to forgive me. You deserved the world, and I could barely give you a whole night with my undivided attention, at least sober."

"So, now you're back for good?" I'm still not sure what his timeframe or intentions are. Is this temporary? Is he trying to get something out of me before heading back to wherever it is he lives now?

"As much as I'd love to say I came back for you, I came back because my mom is dying. She was diagnosed with ovarian cancer about six years ago. It's basically a miracle she's lived this long. But things have gotten worse and quickly. I came back to be with her and to make peace with you. It's time. It's *been* time, and I've been too chicken to do it. But Mom being so sick, well it puts things in perspective in a new way." His eyes glance away for a second, and I know this is what he meant by the frailty of life.

"When I got back to town, I was certain you were going to be married with kids holding on to your pants. But when I found out you weren't?

I swear I nearly fainted. That was the first day I walked into the bakery. I knew it was the three of you from the first time I saw it. It's amazing, Ali. Truly amazing what you've done there, what you've all done. Everybody talks about how amazing the food and coffee is. I'm really proud of you." He's said so much in such a short breath that I have to take a moment to try to focus.

"Wait, go back a bit. Your mom is dying?" The thought alone nearly doubles me over as I digest it. His mom is one of the most amazing women I've ever been lucky enough to know.

"Yeah. The doctors gave her weeks. At most three months, but they said it's a long shot for her to make it to next month."

My heart officially shatters. I loved his mom. Every so often, she'd come into the café and order something. Her eyes were always filled with a level of sadness most wouldn't notice. But I knew her cheeriness, her lively demeanor. And the downturned lips and eyes I got when she came in are not her. They're her pity, her guilt, perhaps. But I haven't seen her in a while.

"I'm sorry, Cam. I had no idea. Sometimes nothing is sacred in this town, and other times secrets are so well kept."

"We wanted it that way. We don't want all the neighbors coming by with casseroles and doting on her. At first, the doctors were optimistic that it'd go into remission, that it was caught early enough, and she was okay for a while, minus her treatments. But now it's back with a vengeance and nothing is working." His chin drops to his chest, and I know it's harder on him than he's going to admit right now.

I, of all people, should know how hard it is to experience a parent dying. And this is a slow and grief-filled process.

"I can understand that. Your mom's always been a more private person. I was surprised she let me in at first."

His head tips back with a loud single laugh and his hand connects with his chest.

"She was definitely hesitant at first. I mean, this gorgeous girl coming to take away her only baby. And from the esteemed Bakers. But she loved you. I'm sure on some level she still does."

We both turn somber as the ramifications from years ago come back.

"I had a nice time tonight, Alina. And I'm happy I finally told you why I left. It was never anything about you. I had a lot to get right and fix with myself, and I stayed away for far too long. But I'm back now. And I want to give this a real try if you're willing."

For all the talk I made about Cameron having to work for it, I'm not making him try very hard. Probably because in the deepest parts of my heart, I don't want to. I want things to be like they were, to go back to the Cameron and Alina we used to be. We may never get there. But I want to try.

"I am. I want that too, I think. I've missed you, Cameron."

His whole face lights up with my words.

Then I sense a hesitation about him. Like he's trying to decide if he should do something. But he seems to choose because he cups my cheek and leans forward, just barely brushing his lips against mine.

It's brief, so brief I almost wonder if it even happened, but it sends tingles racing from my lips through my entire body and a sigh easing from my chest.

More. I want more. More kisses, more hands, more time.

But as he sits back, not giving me more, not indulging in a deeper kiss, I know he's right to take this slow. It's what we need to rebuild our foundation.

"I think I should go before I do something ungentlemanlike." His gaze trails over me, and he clears his throat. "Thank you for dinner, and the conversation. I'll be by the café tomorrow, same time as always, and I look forward to seeing you."

He stands and walks to the door. I'm too stunned to even get up. But he doesn't think anything of it, leaving without another word.

The second he's gone, I'm on my feet and pacing. So much heavy information was just shared. An addiction? His mom's dying? I can barely wrap my head around any of those realities.

But what I choose to focus on is that he wants to try things again. He wants to be with me. I fall back to the couch and kick my feet in the air, giddy and excited. I can't wait for tomorrow.

Chapter 12

Cameron

I can't believe I kissed her. It was the tiniest little peck, but I'm surprised she didn't push me away. My lips have been tingling for days since it happened, and I'm dying to do it again, but the opportunity hasn't presented itself.

I've tried to convince her to let me come into the kitchen with her, as I'd love to watch her work. It used to be one of my favorite pastimes. And not just because I was the official taste tester.

The look of concentration that she gets when she's working is extremely endearing and incredibly sexy. Not to mention the fact that she almost always has flour somewhere on her person. It's adorable that she usually has no idea it's there.

In the days since the kiss, she's spent every one with me while I visit and eat a muffin. A few times she's even grabbed a piece and smiled while eating it. Things are starting to fall back into place, but I need more.

More time, more one-on-one, and far fewer prying eyes.

But she hasn't invited me over again, and I won't be inviting myself like last time. That was rude of me, and I shouldn't have done it. I was just so desperate to tell her what happened.

She took it better than I expected. It's a big deal to tell somebody you have an addiction. Because it's something I'll always have; it will never go away. I just have to be better about how I respond to the impulse to use again.

So far, I've done well for ten years. It was hard when Mom was first diagnosed. I wanted to dive into the first bottle of pills I could find to numb out the pain of hearing that she has cancer. But I called my sponsor, and we got through it together. I barely even drink because it can become a slippery slope, and one vice can become another.

I didn't want to put all that on Alina at once, and when she offered wine with dinner, I didn't want to say no. So I kept it to one glass that I nursed the whole night. She did the same.

Today as I head over to the café, I'm trying to come up with an idea of how to get another night alone with her. I could ask her out on another date, but there are always too many people around.

To get to know Alina again, in this life and not our high school one, I need to see her in action, to see her in her element. And that's always been in the kitchen.

When I get through the door, I immediately notice Alina isn't anywhere to be found, and I wonder if she decided what I told her was too much for her to handle. That she no longer wants to give this a shot. My breaths come faster as my heart races at the thought.

"Alina here today?" There's a tremor to my voice that I hope Liv doesn't pick up on.

"She is. She'll be out in a few minutes. I think she wanted to finish a batch of something new. What can I get you today?" Relief floods me.

There's a touch less animosity in her tone than there usually is, and I'm wondering if Alina has gotten Liv to be on my side again.

"I think I'll try a scone today."

She reaches into the case to grab one, keeping her gaze on me the whole time, but it isn't filled with hatred like normal. There's even a slight smile on her face.

"Alina's been happier, you know. Since you two started talking again."

"That's great to hear."

The plate with the scone on it slams down in front of me. "Know that if you hurt her again, there's nowhere you can hide that we won't find you. All three of us."

I make sure to catch her intent stare in mine. "I want nothing more than to make Alina happy, Liv. I have no intentions of hurting her."

"Did you last time?"

"Fair point. But I'm a different person now, Liv. I was going through something then that I wasn't mature enough to handle. I'm older now and have a firm grasp on it."

"Alina mentioned something." When my eyes widen, she reaches a hand forward. "Without going into specifics. She just said that your reason for leaving was legitimate and that she believes you're here for the right reasons. I love my sister, Cameron. I'm going to be watching you very closely. Hell, the whole town probably is."

"I can understand that. But know I'm not going down without a fight."

"Well, Alina doesn't seem to be putting up much of one. But that doesn't mean you're just welcomed back into the fold. You have to prove yourself to the rest of us." I wonder if Alina told her about the kiss.

"I'll do whatever I have to, to prove to all of you that I'm here for Alina. I want to do things right this time, and I have no intention of going anywhere unless she sends me away."

Her gaze travels over my body like she's sizing me up and wondering if she can trust me. She must decide that she can because she smirks and slides the plate toward me, spinning around to pour my coffee. I like that I'm at the point where I don't need to tell them what kind of coffee I want.

It's that moment that Alina walks through the door, dusting her hands on her apron before taking it off and dropping it on the counter. She turns to me and smiles an all-tooth grin that makes my heart race.

"Hey. Sorry, I was finishing up something in the kitchen." She rounds the counter and brushes her fingers across my back.

"I'd love to come see."

Her head tilts to the side and one corner of her mouth tips down. "You know I can't let you back there, Cameron. Insurance and all that."

I'm sure that it's a load of bullshit, but I won't push. She'll let me back there at some point. "Alright, alright. I'll get back there, Alina, you mark my words."

She rolls her eyes and giggles, jutting her chin toward the mostly empty dining area. Sometimes I wonder how they stay in business, but I likely come at an off time. I've seen swarms here and they have a pretty good tourist business from what Dad says.

I follow her over to our usual table and quickly place my coffee and scone down so I can run around to the other side and hold out her chair for her.

"Why, thank you."

"No coffee for you today?"

"No, it's been keeping me up at night. I don't have the ability to drink it nonstop and bear no side effects like Liv does. Or you, apparently." She gives a nod to my cup as she laces her fingers together on the table.

"It keeps me up sometimes, but I'm dragging through work by the end of the day. Those phone calls are relentless and boring, so I need something to give me a little pep."

"You know, it's a pretty boring coffee order."

My eyes shoot to my hairline. "I'm sorry?"

"It is! Black coffee? We have so many other amazing drinks and all you want is plain coffee."

"It's what I like." I chuckle.

"I think you should spice it up a little. Something fun and fancy."

"Or you come up with a fun and fancy name for a plain black coffee." If it will keep me from having to order some froufrou drink, I'll take it.

"I can't do that."

"You own the café. You can do whatever you want."

Her eyes light up like she's never thought of that before. "Okay. I'll come up with something."

"Looking forward to it." I shake my head and smile. This is the sort of silly thing she always used to do.

"How's your mom doing?" Her lip pulls between her teeth, like she's not sure she should be asking.

"She's hanging in. I don't know what to do with the situation. She seems ready, prepared. I can't say the same about Dad. He seems to find a new hobby every weekend to keep his mind off of it." I sigh at the thought. The garage is so full of junk and clutter that you can't even fit a car in it anymore.

Her hand closes over mine. "And you? How are you handling it?"

"As good as can be expected, I suppose. In a lot of ways, I kind of try to avoid thinking it's the end and that she's just sick still. But the reality is far more glum. It's just hard to face and even harder to accept."

"I can't imagine." Her voice trails off until it's barely a whisper.

And I want to smack myself. Because Alina's dealt with far worse. She lost both parents, and it wasn't a long time coming. There was nothing she could do to prepare for the loss. While I know she'd argue and tell me loss is loss, I have time to grieve before having to face the facts. I have time to wrap my head around the idea of a world without my mother, even if I have no clue what that actually looks like.

Alina didn't have that luxury.

"I had a nice time at dinner the other night. Thanks again for having me over." A change of subject is a good idea right now.

"You're welcome. I had a nice time too. It was good to be able to talk, just us."

"I'll be honest, I was a little worried when you weren't out here when I came in today. I thought maybe what I shared was too much for you." I look down at my plate and break off a piece of scone to pop in my mouth. Of course it's just as delicious as everything Alina makes. I'm pretty sure she could take all my least favorite foods and turn them into something I'd devour.

"I was just finishing up a new recipe. I'm sorry, I didn't mean to worry you."

"I'd understand, you know. If it was too much to handle. It's a lot, and it's not something that will ever go away, just something I have to keep control of." Being vulnerable is not something that tends to come easily to me, but it always has with Alina.

"I'd be lying if I said I wasn't worried about it, but I meant it when I said I was willing to give this a try, Cameron. While I don't necessarily

know exactly what that entails with your addiction, I'm willing to learn."
Her words wrap me in a blanket of security. Of all the things I've shared
with her, this is the one that could turn her away forever, which is why I
never told her in the first place.

I never intended to be away so long. And when I came back to hear she
was likely getting engaged, it nearly drove me back to the pills. I figured
there wasn't a point anymore. I couldn't tell her that. I couldn't let her
think she would be a reason for my relapse. Because really, I'm my own
reason. It all falls on my shoulders, each and every time. It was my fault
in the beginning, and it would be my fault in the event of a relapse.

With time and practice, I've been able to seek help when I need it. I've
been able to stay strong so far. Alina just gives me a reason to stay that
way.

Chapter 13
Alina

Cameron's presence in the kitchen is becoming more routine, and more comfortable. No longer do I shrink away under his watchful eye. I'd always loved having him keep me company while I whipped something up, but I was sure after all this time, and the hurt, it would never feel right again.

I was wrong.

While I'm not sure he bought my reasoning to keep him out, like insurance, he didn't argue it.

Until the day he saw Liv and Jay leaving the kitchen. Of course they'd be the ones to ruin it for me. When I tried to argue that he was only helping her carry out trays of food, he wasn't actually *in* the kitchen, Cameron gave me the look he has when he knows I'm full of shit, with his head tilted to the side and one corner of his mouth tipped down.

After that, I couldn't deny his entry, and he's become a permanent staple to my nightly prep. Often here most mornings too.

Tonight, as he leans his hip against the counter, arms crossed over his broad chest with a light smile gracing his face, I can't help the quirk of my lips and the flutter in my chest as I mix the batter.

"What's so funny?" His eyes narrow as he asks, his smile widening, and he reaches out to grab a raspberry before popping it into his mouth.

"Nothing, I just...I like having you here."

The realization is a little hard to swallow. This man, I loved him so completely, but he caused so much hurt. I have to remember to guard my heart because he could leave without a trace again. I've had every intention of doing so, and yet, every day I notice how much he seeps in like he was never gone. I care for him more than I thought I would just two months after reconciling. Not to mention all the light kissing we've been doing that has me begging for so much more.

"I like being here. I've always enjoyed watching you cook. It's almost like a performance. You're graceful and dynamic, comfortable." When he's quiet, I look up and find his gaze intently on me, making heat rush my face. "Do you remember that time you tried to make me caramels?"

"Yes! I tried to make them because they're your favorite. I still have the scar to prove my efforts."

Before I can even respond, he closes the space between us and runs his thumb along the discolored skin. An electric current prickles up my arm and throughout my body. Of course I don't have to remind him where it is. At one time, he knew the map of my body so well, possibly better than I did.

"They're my favorite because they're the same color as your eyes, Ali." One hand cups my cheek, his thumb rubbing under my eye while his fingers tighten around my wrist, just over my burn scar.

There's such magnetism between us you can practically see the waves pulsating. That was never the issue, it still isn't.

All at once, Cam loops an arm around my waist and cups my cheek, yanking me against him so our chests meet and our lips crash. Whatever tether has been holding both of us from each other just snapped, and the pieces lay broken on the floor.

His mouth is powerful against my own, pushing it open as his tongue slips in to curl against mine. This isn't the sweet, tender kissing we've been dipping our toes into. This is raw, real, unrestrained, and filled with years' worth of emotions.

Fast fingers slip under the hem of my shirt and pull it off before reaching behind Cam's shoulders to do the same to his. The hunger that swirls through his eyes is enough to turn my panties to ash.

Caught in his intense stare, I don't even know that he's unhooked my bra until he's sliding it off my arms. His large hands immediately cup my breasts, and I suck air through my teeth as cool skin meets warmth, like ice meeting fire.

Running his thumbs over my nipples, he takes two steps toward me, forcing me to take two back until my spine hits the edge of the counter.

We're in the kitchen at the café, and if Mazie ever found out what we were doing, what I'm *fairly* certain we're going to do, she'd have my head on a platter and serve it as the next day's special. But now that we've started this dance, I know there's no stopping it.

Sliding his hands down my body, he flips the button on my jeans, lowering them and pulling them from body. A slight tremble settles into my bones, and I grip the edge of the counter to keep myself upright.

Cameron trails his fingertips up my legs, his gaze following as he bites his bottom lip. "I've been thinking about this for a long time now, Alina."

There's no opportunity to answer before he closes his mouth over mine, losing his hand in my hair and swiping his tongue along the seam of my lips. I'm not sure if I was going to tell him the truth, that I've been thinking about it too.

Strong hands close around my hips, and he lifts me onto the edge, spreading my thighs and stepping between them. My palms rest just above his chest, almost hovering instead of touching, like I'm nervous to actually feel his skin against mine.

A devilish look appears across his face as he breaks the kiss and reaches to dip his fingers into the bowl behind me. Putting his finger to my lips, he trails it down my chin, to the top of my rib cage and down between my breasts, smearing chocolate frosting on his way.

Without skipping a beat, he leans forward, licking the frosting off until he meets my lips. When he pulls away, his thumb immediately wipes some chocolate from the corner of my lips, which he then pulls to his own.

The desire burning in his eyes is enough to scorch my skin, and I'm almost afraid I'm going to burst into flames under his intense stare.

Instead, he shifts his focus back to the bowl, dipping his fingers in again. This time, he rubs the chocolate over my nipples and my head tips back. When he closes his lips around one, my hand flies to the back of his head, my fingers tangling in his hair.

The second I wrap my legs around his waist, he tugs me closer, and his erection presses right against my throbbing clit. He runs his palms up my thighs, and my fingers fumble as I try to hurriedly undo his jeans.

Unhooking my legs, he takes a step back and steps out of his pants. The second he's standing between my legs again, I wrap my arms around his neck and pull him against me, causing him to stumble slightly. When he catches himself by planting his hands on the table behind me, he hits a bowl of dry ingredients, sending them puffing all over us.

The coughing and laughter are short lived once we lock eyes. Cameron pounces on me so fast it steals my air. Sliding his hand between our bodies, he slips along my wetness and growls deep in his chest before plunging two fingers inside me and pulling a moan from my lips.

"Cam."

"Fuck, Ali. I've waited so long to hear you say my name like that again."

Any other words are lost in my throat as he hooks his fingers and flicks his tongue along my pebbled nipple.

I'm about to come when he removes his fingers and straightens up, cupping my face and sweeping his tongue into my mouth as he presses his cock into me.

A choked "fuck" leaves his lips once he's all the way inside me. If I could even utter a sound, I'd echo his sentiment.

With his hands tight on my hips, Cameron starts thrusting into me, hard and fast. The table shifts and creaks with our movements. So much so, that a bowl has moved itself closer, and I don't realize until I move my hand back to anchor myself and tip my top half back. Doing so, my hand hits the edge of the bowl and I send it flying, dousing us in cold batter.

But Cam doesn't hesitate, doesn't slow. Batter drips from his ear, but he's still fucking me like it's his sole purpose in life.

Sliding a hand up my back, he tangles it in my hair, pulling it back so he can lick up my neck and along the shell of my ear.

"Do you know how long I've wanted to fuck you in a kitchen, Alina? It's when you're at your most stunning, most confident. It's incredibly sexy and makes me hard as fuck every time." The words come out slightly fractured through the movement, a little breathless, and somewhat distant due to the blood whooshing in my ears.

If I wanted to be honest, with him and myself, I'd tell him that I've always fantasized about this very thing, ever since an almost situation in culinary school. I stopped when he came too close because the thoughts of Cameron had still been strong. My fantasy started with him, and if I have it my way, it'll end with him.

"I'd love to flip you over this table and fuck you from behind like I know you like, Ali, but I want to watch you come. Are you going to do that for me, baby?"

"Yes." Every stroke of his rock-hard cock inside me sends pulsations ricocheting through me. He doesn't realize I'm standing on the precipice, ready to fall. Or maybe he does.

Leaning forward, he licks up my neck, along a track of batter. "Mm, this batter tastes deliciously sweet, Ali. Just like I remember you tasting."

As he talks, he slides his hand forward, his thumb pressing against my clit. Straightening up, he watches me with a parted mouth and starts swirling his finger.

My nails dig into the back of his neck and scratch down his chest as I tighten around him, tip my head back, and fill the kitchen with the sound of his name.

Slowing but not stopping, he continues to fuck me through the tremors until I'm still. Then he pulls me off the counter, supports under my thighs, and presses me against the fridge.

At the sudden iciness against my back, my spine peels away, my breasts grazing his perfect abs.

One of his hands holds me up, while the other grips the top of the fridge, and he plows into me relentlessly. If the fridge wasn't so big, and wasn't so firmly in place, I'm sure it'd be rattling. I'm only hoping that the contents inside are just as sturdy, or the Prater's wedding cake may not be as perfect as it was when I put it in earlier today.

Having to stay up all night and remake the cake would be worth every second of this euphoric, orgasmic bliss, though.

It takes all of five more thrusts for Cam to groan into my neck. After slowing his way through his release, he rests his forehead against the cool metal behind me, both of us breathing heavily. A quick glance around the kitchen shows me it's an absolute disaster, as are we, slick with sweat and sticky in random spots.

Burying his head in my neck, his lips press against my tingling skin before he gently sets me down.

"We're filthy. And in *so* much trouble if Mazie ever finds out." The thought of Mazie knowing sends a chill racing down my spine.

"Let's make sure she doesn't." With a quick peck on the tip of my nose, he turns around at the crime scene behind us and starts laughing.

I smack his chest. "It's not funny, Cam. We need to clean this up. And take a shower."

"*A* shower?" He turns back toward me with a quirked eyebrow.

"You know what I mean." Though suddenly the idea of Cam in my shower is extremely enticing.

Apparently to both of us, as he steps closer, pressing his pelvis to mine, and slides his hands up my sides. "What can I do to convince you to let me join you?"

"Nothing."

His hands and face both drop, and he takes a step back. But I follow, pressing my body to his and putting my fingers under his chin, pushing up so his eyes meet mine.

"There's nothing you can do or say because I was already going to ask you to join me. Come home with me, Cam. I'm yours, if you still want me. No more games."

This game of hard-to-get was getting tiresome, especially because I was punishing myself just as much as Cam.

When he doesn't respond or flinch, a cold wisp starts to tangle around my heart. Until his smile breaks so widely across his face, and he loops his arm around my waist, gently tucking hair behind my ear with the other.

"I want you, Ali. All I want is you. All I've *ever* wanted, is you. I may have lost sight of that when I got tangled up in the pills. But if I've known one thing, it's that I love you and plan to for the rest of my life."

I open my mouth to say something in response, but he presses a kiss to my lips instead.

"Don't."

"Don't what?"

"Don't say anything. I've never stopped loving you, Alina. I know that. But you had a life, and you were the one who was hurt, so I don't want you saying it back until you're sure you mean it, and I don't think we're there yet. I'm okay with that fact." He runs a thumb along my lip, then leans down and pulls it between his teeth. "But I think we'll get there."

"Come home with me. Come home with me and spend the night." I trail my fingers up his deliciously naked chest, leaving a trail through the flour that doused us earlier.

He hooks his hands under my thighs and lifts me again. "I'd be happy to."

Carrying me over to the counter, he sets me down again. I take a real look around. We're both stark naked in the kitchen of the café. I'm eternally thankful that Jameson took Liv down to the city this weekend and that Mazie doesn't check in on me at night. It's just us, the only lights the ones glowing above us.

We quickly redress and begin cleaning. He stays close behind me the whole time, his fingers grazing over my body every few minutes. We're able to wrap up and make the kitchen at least presentable, organized, and sanitized for tomorrow morning.

The dry ingredients, batter, and frosting are all cleaned up and put away, aside from on our bodies.

"Come on, let's go clean ourselves." Taking his hand, I tug him out the door, shutting off the lights and locking everything up behind me.

Chapter 14

Cameron

I follow Alina back to her house. Part of me is still reeling from the fact that I just got to fuck her in the kitchen. And hopefully will get to do it again and again as I lie beside her tonight.

The second I park, I'm out of the car, my hands wrapping around her waist, and I'm waiting impatiently while she opens the door. My breath is hot on her neck, and she giggles as my thumbs slide under the waistband of her jeans.

I was starving for her, and now that I've had her once again, there's no stopping things. I just hope she's as hungry for me.

The second we're through the threshold, I'm spinning her around and throwing her up against the door, my hips pressing into her as my mouth latches onto her neck.

"Cam." It comes out half giggle, half choked breath.

My hands plant on either side of her head, but she's too quick and scoots out from under me with a laugh, grabbing my wrist and pulling me wordlessly farther into the house.

Once we're in the bathroom, she lets go of my hand, leaning into the shower to turn on the water. The bathroom immediately starts to fill with steam, and she spins around, placing her fingers under the hem of my shirt and lifting.

That's when I take over, reaching behind my head and tearing the garment from my body before my hands dive to hers and lift it, immediately wrapping around her back to unhook her bra, and gently removing it from her body.

I press her against the wall, and air hisses through her teeth as her back arches away from the cold tile. I palm her breasts and take her pebbling nipples between my thumbs and forefingers. Her fingers trail down my chest to rest against the top of my jeans.

Leaning down, I pull one of her nipples into my mouth, and her arms wrap around my head, one leg lifting to circle my waist. I lower my hands to lift her and lave at her nipple with my tongue.

Then I climb into the shower.

Alina yelps as water pounds down on us.

"Cameron! Our pants."

"Good point." I set her down and immediately remove the soaking bottoms from her body, shucking mine off next. They sit soaking on the shower floor, but all I can think about is Alina and having her again. All of her, more of her. Never enough of her.

Closing the gap between us, she backs against the wall, and I have to tilt my head down to look at her. She's everything I've wanted, and she's finally back where she belongs, trapped by my body and mine again.

I run my fingertips up her arms, down her chest, around her waist, anywhere they can reach. It's like I'm trying to memorize the feel of her skin, the map of her body. The whole time, she looks up at me with wide eyes and parted lips.

I take her bottom lip between my teeth and slide my tongue into her mouth to move against hers. She moans into my mouth as my cock presses against her thigh.

Very briefly the thought of birth control came to mind in the kitchen, but not enough for me to care. Alina having my baby would be the greatest thing ever, and something I hope for someday. But she didn't bring it up either, so I'm sure we're protected in some way. If it's anything like before, she's still on the pill.

My knee presses between her thighs, and she parts them even farther and grinds against me, telling me she's ready for me. God, she's so damn sexy.

The water pelts against my back as I box her against the wall, her chest heaving in anticipation.

I slide my hand down her body so my fingers can slip along her soaking pussy. A shudder runs through me as I think about fucking her again.

Two fingers dip inside her, and I hook them immediately, stroking at that bundle of nerves that will push her over the edge. Her head tips back against the tiles, and her hands grip at my shoulders while her hips push toward me.

My mouth latches to hers, and I press my tongue through her lips. Every moan and whimper, I swallow down, storing in a place deep inside me.

I kiss along her collarbone, settling against her ear. "Come for me, baby. Tell me how good it feels. Let me hear your voice. I know you like to talk dirty, so tell me."

"Fuck, Cam. It feels so good. Don't stop, please. I'm so fucking close." Her eyes are pinched shut, and I pull her earlobe between my teeth.

She yelps and bucks her hips against my hand. My thumb finds her clit and starts making pressurized circles and she turns to putty in my hands.

Her legs nearly give out and her body starts to shudder as her nails drag down my back and she screams my name.

"Good girl, Ali. Now I want—fuck." She reads my mind and takes my dick in her hand, her grip firm as she glides it up and down my rock-hard length. My head faces the ceiling with a groan.

And then she gets to her knees and replaces her hand with her perfect mouth, pulling me in as far as she can. Her tongue swirls around the head of my cock as she bobs forward and backward, my fingers fisting into her hair. I hold her still and start fucking her mouth, her moans of approval pushing me harder and faster.

But I don't want to come down her throat. So I pull out of her, despite her trying to grab at my ass to take me back. Wrapping my hands around her biceps, I pull her to stand, spin her around, and push her shoulders down so her back is arched, and her ass is sticking up in the air.

I run my hands over the swell of her ass before lining myself up and gliding the tip of my hard cock along her soaking pussy. The temperature of the shower is something I've lost sight of. The water pulsating down on my body is no more than a nuisance as all I can focus on is diving into Alina again.

Bending over her back, I press my lips to her ear. "You suck my dick so good, baby. But let's see how you take it."

"Mmm, let me show you." She pushes her ass back against me.

"Fuck. So greedy."

"I've had you once, it wasn't enough. I need you again, Cam." Her hands plant on the wall in front of her and she pushes back to look at me.

Without another word, I slam into her in one fell swoop. One deep thrust and I'm all the way inside her, both of our breaths catching with a moan.

"Fuck, baby. You're so tight and wet I can barely stand it."

All she does is whimper in response. My hands wrap tightly around her hips, and I start thrusting hard and fast into her. Her body jerks forward with the movement, and her cheek rests against her hand, mouth parted and eyes closed tightly.

As she stays bent over, and I keep slamming into her, the water pools between us and sloshes with every thrust. It's distracting me from my mission and adding an annoyance to the situation.

I pull out and spin her to face me, wrapping my hands under her thighs and lifting her up so she loops her legs around my waist. I back her against the wall and resume drilling into her.

"You're so fucking sexy, Alina." The words come out broken between harsh breaths.

"Do I take your dick good?"

"Oh, like such a good girl. You're a pro at taking my dick, though. Aren't you?"

Even from the beginning, it's like our bodies have always been made for each other. At first, I remember her being nervous, which is normal, but more about that I wouldn't fit than anything else. She didn't mention it at all this time, probably because she remembers that even if it's tight, it's incredible.

Bending, I pull her nipple between my teeth and clamp down, eliciting a shriek as she grabs onto my head and yanks my hair. As I lavish her nipple with my tongue, she starts to shudder.

"Fuck, Cam. I'm going to come. Don't stop."

"That's it, baby. Come for me. Right on my dick."

Three more hard thrusts and she tightens around me. It sets off my own orgasm and I pulsate deep inside her. I give a few more slow pushes into her before lowering her to her feet and resting my forehead against the cool tile.

"Well, that wasn't the point of this shower."

"Not worth it?"

"I didn't say that." A smirk tugs up one corner of her mouth as she reaches around me to adjust the water.

"Can I wash you?"

Without answering, she hands me a loofah and adds body wash. "Just don't get it on my hair, okay?"

"I remember." My voice is low and quiet. She takes good care of her curls, and part of that is not letting certain things on it, including body wash and soap.

The hard part in all of this is that it's new and old at the same time. We're learning new things about each other, learning how we've changed over time, but there's still so much to remember and so many things we've experienced before.

Taking the loofah, I start gently scrubbing her arms, then her chest, then crouching to wash her legs. I press a kiss right to her pussy before running the loofah over it. I work up her stomach back to her chest and spend a little extra time at her breasts. My cock hardens again, but the next time I fuck this woman it's going to be in a bed.

Once I finish her front, I guide her under the water to rinse so I can flip her hair over her shoulder and scrub her back.

I let her finish rinsing and grab the body wash, squeezing some into my hand and quickly lathering myself up. She stands back while I rinse and watches as I give myself a few rough strokes.

"Hey. That's my job." Stepping forward, she swats my hand away and takes me in her palm. My head drops with a groan as she slides her hand firmly up and down my shaft.

But she quickly lets go, her tongue poking out of the corner of her mouth. Somehow, I forgot she can be such a little tease.

"Towels?"

"Closet."

Without another word, I step out of the shower and wrap myself in a big fluffy teal towel, grabbing a pink one and holding it out to Alina as she turns off the water and steps into it.

I wrap her in it before looping my arms around her and pulling her against my chest, swaying slightly.

"I love you."

She turns in my grasp, having to fight against me because my hold on her is so strong. "I know you don't want me to say it yet, but I love you, Cam. I do. I'm not sure I ever really stopped."

My heart races faster than ever at her words, and I bend to pick her up and throw her over my shoulder. I carry her out of the bathroom right into her room and toss her on the bed. She giggles as she falls back and stretches wide, her towel opening as she does.

For somebody who was so shy about my being in the kitchen with her at first, she certainly has no shame about showing off her body to me. And damn is it a great body.

"You're perfect. Do you know that?"

"I'm far from it, Cam. Trust me, we all have demons." What possible demons could she have? I know of the big ones; I was here when they happened. What could be worse than that?

"Either way, you're perfect for me."

She sits up, going to her dresser and pulling out some clothes. As she tosses a few things my way, I quirk an eyebrow.

"They're Eli's."

"Oh, well won't he just want to burn them after knowing I've touched them? How come he hasn't come to beat me to a pulp yet?"

She saunters over and stands between my legs where I sit on the bed, a long shirt now covering her. "Because I asked him not to. He hasn't come to say hi either because he's not sure he can control himself just yet. But I've told him we're on a good path, Cam. That I want to give this a shot and he's trying to be respectful of that."

"I appreciate that. But if you don't mind, I'd rather just sleep naked."

She giggles and holds a hand over her mouth. "That's fine too. I'd join you, but I tend to get cold at night."

Grabbing her wrist, I yank her into my lap. "I'm here to keep you warm."

Biting her lip, she looks down at her legs, then back up at me with a smile. She quickly jumps off my lap and climbs to the top of the bed, where she pulls back the covers and pats the spot next to her.

I settle under the covers and sidle up behind her, turning her to her side and pulling her into my chest. Wrapping myself around her, I hold her close and rest my chin on her shoulder. She fits so perfectly in my little bubble.

She always has. Even though we've both grown a bit since high school, we still fit.

Alina is my other half, my puzzle piece. And this time, I plan to stick around.

Chapter 15
Alina

The smile hasn't left my face since last night. It's the first real night of sleep I've had in ages. Something about having Cam there made me feel safe and protected. Not a single nightmare reared its ugly head.

For the first time in a long time, I feel rested. And happy.

To the point that I'm humming to myself as I frost some cupcakes for a birthday party when Liv storms into the kitchen.

She marches right over to the big garbage can, grips both sides, and pukes into it. My eyes widen, and I put down my materials to go rub her back.

"Sibby? Do you need to go home? Are you sick?"

"No. Well, yes. I'm pregnant." My eyes widen even farther, though I'm not sure it's possible, and my mouth forms a perfect 'O'.

"You're *pregnant*? Does Jameson know?"

She grips the sides of the can tighter and turns over her shoulder to look at me, her face pale and clammy. "Of course he does." There's snarkiness to her tone that I don't appreciate.

"Alright, down girl."

"Sorry. It's been a rough several weeks."

"Several? How many are we talking?"

Her shoulders rise to her ears as she cringes. "Ten."

"You're *ten* weeks pregnant and I am just now finding out? What the fuck, Olivia?" Righteous indignation rises within me. We're supposed to be sisters, and beyond that, best friends.

"Jameson wanted to wait. I only found out a few weeks ago because you know my period can be off schedule. So I waited and then it was beyond late so I tested. It was a huge shock. I didn't start getting sick until a week or two ago."

"Isn't morning sickness supposed to wean off over time?" When Cameron and I started being sexually active in high school, I learned all about pregnancy; the signs, the symptoms, the whole nine yards.

"The doctor said it can last into the second trimester, which is soon. It hasn't been too bad, but when it sneaks up on me, boy, does it get to me." She straightens and wipes her mouth, walking over to the fridge and pulling out a bottle of water, which she opens and swishes some in her mouth, then spits into the garbage.

"I'm sorry, Sibby. It sounds rough. Sheesh, you and Jameson don't mess around." They had a few months' long engagement and have been married for five months now. Not very much time together before moving on to the next step.

She waves a hand at me as if to dismiss the thought. "Why wait? We're happily married and in love. Why put it off? Though it wasn't exactly planned. But seriously, why put off your own happiness because of a timetable?"

"Yeah, I'm starting to see the good reasoning behind that."

"Ah, you mean with Cam. How are things going between you two?" She takes another swill of water and recaps the bottle, giving me a knowing look.

"They're going really well actually." My face heats as I think of just how well they went last night in this very kitchen.

"He's certainly putting in the time and effort. I'm happy you're happy, Leen. Just...be careful with him."

I take a deep breath to tamp down the fire that's started in my stomach. I know she's just being protective of me in regard to the past with Cameron, but I wish they'd all trust me. "I am, Liv."

"Good, good. Okay. I think the wave has passed. I'm going to go back out to the floor since the lunch rush is coming. You need anything?"

"Nope, I'm good. I'll be out to help with the sandwiches and things as soon as I finish this batch for the Leivish's birthday party." On top of just our day-to-day fare of treats and sandwiches, I also take on cakes and cupcakes here and there.

With a nod, she goes back through the door, through which I immediately hear the bell chime and know she has to put on her happy hostess act. How we decided Liv should be front of house, I have no idea. She can be friendly enough, but it's not natural to her and must be draining, especially with how she's feeling now.

Mazie swears she's so busy running the back end, yet she's never here. I have no idea what she really does with her time, but it's rarely spent at her place of business. For all we really know, she's kicking back and relaxing, handling phone calls when they come up and placing orders.

It helps that we have such a small staff. It's myself, Liv, and then a few other girls. Stacey is probably the most competent of the crew and stood in for Liv while she was both out with her injury and on her honeymoon.

I can't believe Liv's pregnant. I wonder what Mazie will say. Surely, she'll say something about the fact that it's fast. That's just how Mazie is.

And it will, without a doubt, piss Liv right off. Which is how their relationship seems to go. Mazie, of course, isn't our mother, but she's the closest thing we have, and I swear she and Liv have that mother-daughter relationship of loving each other but getting on one another's last nerve in the same breath.

I worry more that Mazie is going to be jealous. She's really wanted to be a mother for as long as I can remember. While it seemed to take a minute, she was okay that Liv got married first, finally accepting Jameson and seeing what we all saw already; that he was good for her.

But a baby? That's a very different story. Not to mention, Mazie's getting older and over thirty. While I don't really consider that old, she does.

If only she'd open her eyes and see how much Zach wants her. She refutes the notion every single time. Life would be so much easier if they didn't try to deny it anymore.

I heard the rumblings from people, wondering if I cared that Liv was getting married before me. I didn't, I don't. Liv and I are close enough in age that it doesn't bother me, but more than that, I'm happy for her. She's my best friend, and I want all of life's good things for her.

Wiping my hands, I set the cupcakes in their boxes and put them in the fridge while they await pick up before walking into the café.

It's bustling, like it usually is during the lunch rush. Kids from the local high school and tons of people working in the area frequent here for lunch. We mostly just have pastries, but we make some mean paninis, wraps, and bagel sandwiches too.

Those are things we order in, the bread products. While I could make them myself, it's just too big of an operation for only me to handle. The muffins, cupcakes, cookies, and other pastries, though, those change daily and are all my creations.

It's exhausting, but I love every second of it. I get to use all my skills and hobbies to make a career. The kitchen is my safe space, it always has been, and now I get to make a living off it.

The only thing missing is the life that Liv has. The husband and soon-to-be family to go home to. I want those things too. For a long time, I was sure I'd never have them because the person I wanted them with left long ago, and nobody else measured up.

But now that Cam's back, I'm not so sure. I only wonder if he wants them too. And with me.

Chapter 16
Cameron

I t's been six weeks since Alina told me she loved me, and I never get tired of hearing it. I've all but moved into her place, spending practically every night with her.

Not only is it everything I've wanted, but it helps distract me from Mom.

She's made it longer than the doctors thought she would, but she's dwindling away. I can see it, and I know she can feel it because she's told me as much. Now, instead of spending a little time each day with Alina, I spend the better part of my day with her and a little time with Mom.

Today, she's feeling peppier and wants to go do something. I don't think it's the best idea, but she insists on me taking her to the café.

"Mom, I don't know about this." We're already in the car and halfway there when I broach the subject again. She looks so small in the seat next to me, her handkerchief over her head with no shame at all.

When somebody asked if she wanted a wig, she scoffed at them. What's happening to her body is terrible, but it's a natural part of her life and she's going to embrace every second by loving her body as it changes.

That's how Mom has always been. It's why I think she's accepted her fate so easily.

"Nonsense, Cameron. I'm feeling good today, and I'd like to get out of the house. Plus, you and Alina are serious again. You're spending most of your time with her. I'd like to see her again."

My jaw tenses, and my grip on the wheel tightens, but I don't argue with her, driving the last two minutes in silence.

When we get to the café, I can see it's thankfully in a lull. I'm not sure Mom could handle the hustle and bustle of how busy it gets to be here at certain times. I hop out of the car, and hurry around to Mom's side to help her out. She takes my hands and lets me steady her as she gets to her feet.

A heavy sigh pulls from her chest as she looks up at the shop. "I wish I came here more often. They say it's the best coffee in town, though I'm much more of a tea person myself."

"They have tea too, Mom."

"Oh, wonderful." With slow and steady footsteps, we walk arm in arm inside. She feels frailer, less sure on her feet. There's a weakness about her that I've never seen before. It sets a sting behind my eyes. But I quickly swallow it down as we enter the café, where I immediately set Mom up at a table. I don't like the idea of her standing too long while we order.

"What kind of tea do you want?"

"Some green tea would be lovely. And I'll let you pick a pastry for me. But please do have Alina come over. I'd like to say hello."

"Of course, Mom."

I give her a quick squeeze on the shoulder before going over to the counter. Neither of the girls are here, so I head back to the kitchen and knock as I swing the door open.

"Hey, ladies."

"Cam!" Alina comes running over and throws her arms around my shoulders. "You're here early today."

"Actually, I'm not alone. There's somebody who wants to see you."

One eyebrow quirks at that. "Oh?"

"Mom."

Her eyes widen and sparkle, all warm and gooey caramel. "Ah. Well, I'd be happy to eat with you both today."

One thing that's always been amazing about Alina is that I can talk about my parents, say Mom and Dad, can even see them and spend time with them, without having a meltdown. I know at first it was hard for her, but she had always loved my parents and looked at them as a second set to her own. I love that she's been able to keep that distinction.

Though maybe I spoke too soon, as she takes a deep breath before we walk through the door to the kitchen.

"Let me grab a few things, and I'll bring them over to the table."

"Okay. Mom asked for a green tea."

"On it!" Liv chimes in from behind us. I hadn't realized she followed us through the door. She busies herself by starting to make the three drinks.

I head back over to the table, sitting next to Mom, leaving room for Alina to sit across from her. "Everything will be right over."

Mom seems distracted, looking out the window with a hard line at her mouth. Following her gaze, I see nothing out of the ordinary. Just a few people strolling by in small-town Juniper Grove. Honestly, I'm kind of surprised there's anybody out there.

"You okay, Mom?"

She turns back to me, and her smile widens, her eyes giving what little light still exists. "Of course, dear."

While I'm sure she's lying, I don't press. She's been doing this more and more lately, which makes me worry the end is getting closer, and that she knows it.

"Hello, Mrs. Dillard."

Mom smiles and moves to stand, but Alina puts her hand out. "Oh, please don't stand for me. I'm nobody special." If that were true, we wouldn't be here right now.

"Nonsense, child. And since when am I Mrs. Dillard? Barbara, please."

"It's good to see you again, Barbara."

"You too, Alina. It's been too long, and I'm sorry I haven't been in more frequently. But once Cameron here told me you two reignited, well, I had to come by before it's too late."

Alina and I exchange a weighted glance. I've told her that Mom is straightforward about dying, that she doesn't hold back, but it's different to hear it in person.

"Oh! I brought some treats. We have a chocolate and caramel muffin, a blueberry scone, and my personal favorite, some biscotti. And Liv will be over with the drinks any minute."

"Liv is here too?" Mom turns around, craning her neck to catch a glimpse. "Ah, yes. She's so grown up now. I always forget about the pink hair."

"Yes, that's Liv's signature these days. Though, at one point not too long ago, she gave purple a shot." Alina giggles, and it lights my heart on fire.

As if summoned, Liv comes over with three steaming mugs and a giant smile. "Hello, Mrs. Dillard. It's nice to see you again. Here's your green tea."

"You too, dear. Love the hair. I wish I had been brave enough to try that at one point in my youth. It looks wonderful on you."

With a fluff of her hair, Liv says 'thank you' and disappears.

"How come she gets to call you Mrs. Dillard?" Alina prods.

"Because she's not dating my only son. You, on the other hand, are once again romantically involved, and that comes with a certain level of intimacy between the families and with names." Mom lifts the mug to her mouth and takes a sip. "Mmm, this is delicious. Who is your supplier?"

Alina's eyes widen, and she sets her mug down from the sip she was about to take. "Oh, I have no idea. That's Mazie's department. I'm sure I could find out for you, if you like."

Mom waves a hand in the air as if to dismiss the thought. "No point. Not much time left to enjoy."

We exchange another glance, and I can feel myself frowning.

"Mom, maybe no more morbid talk for the rest of the conversation?"

"Well, then whatever will we talk about?" She laughs a heartier laugh than I've heard in months.

This whole situation is difficult. Mom is very open and honest about dying, but it's a fine line between what Alina can handle and what she can't. Or at least it used to be.

"I love what you have here, Alina. It's the talk of the town, always. Everybody swears by your bakery for any event, and they talk about how wonderful the coffee is. It's truly remarkable." She takes a sip of her tea as she eyes Alina over the rim of the mug.

Alina's cheeks pink as she tucks a chocolate curl behind her ear, her hands wrapping around her cup. I put my hand on her knee under the table to calm her as she's now clearly embarrassed, though she has no reason to be. "Thank you. It's a team effort, really. I'd be nowhere without Liv and Mazie. Even Eli."

"How are they? Your family?"

Alina cringes at the word. It's so slight, so subtle, I'm sure Mom didn't even notice. But I did. It causes me to squeeze her thigh.

"They're great. Liv's married, though I'm sure you've heard that through the grapevine this town is so well known for. Mazie seems great. She's still so guarded around us, it's hard to know. And Eli, while he's pretty aloof, living out in Pineville City and all that, he's still the big brother we know and love." Her face absolutely lights up when she talks about them. It's impossible to miss how much she loves her siblings. All three of them.

"I did hear Liv was married. How lovely for her. I've seen them around town together. He's quite a looker."

"Mom!" I sink in my seat and groan.

"What? I can acknowledge the good looks of other men and be happily married to your father. And don't worry, dear, you're still the best-looking man in my mind." She pats my cheek like I'm a child and my face burns.

Alina giggles next to me, and when I shoot her a look, surely all daggers, she pulls her lips into her mouth and takes a sip of her coffee.

Mom laughs too, but it's short-lived, and she turns somber. "Now I know I agreed to no more morbid talk, but it's the reality I'm faced with right now. I'm dying; there's no way around that fact. I'm surprised I've lasted as long as I have since the diagnosis." She looks between the two of us, likely to make sure we're not going to argue with this newest topic of conversation.

"I wanted to come here today to see you again, Alina, because while it's been a while since I've been to the café, it's been even longer since I've seen you as Cam's girlfriend."

"Mo—" She stops me by holding up a single finger.

"Do not interrupt me, young man. I will say what I need to." She gives me a firm look, and I sit back in my seat, resigned to listening.

Alina doesn't say a word, but she puts her hand over mine and laces our fingers together in a show of solidarity.

"You're back in each other's lives and I, for one, think it's wonderful. I wasn't happy about the way things happened, and several times since then, I wished I could take it back and change it. Alina, so many times I wanted to tell you what happened, but I didn't feel it was my explanation to give. Then time just kept passing and it felt too late. I'm glad you've found your way back and are together again." She looks between the two of us, but I can't take my eyes off her. Where is she going with this?

"I know it's traditional for the man to ask the woman's father for permission to get married, but—"

"Mom. We're nowhere near getting married. This conversation is premature."

"Don't you understand, Cameron? There is no other time." There's an anger and forcefulness to her tone that I barely recognize.

She stares me down for a second before turning back to Alina. "I wanted to say, that I give my blessing. Whether you two find a way to get there or not, know you have my blessing since I won't be around to give it when you need it."

We sit in silence for a moment, nobody really sure what to say. But then Alina reaches her hand onto the table, taking Mom's and squeezing. "Thank you, Barbara. That means more to me than you can ever know."

Mom flips her hand over and wraps Alina's in hers. They share a look, and something passes between them, something I'll likely never know or understand. Mom wipes away a stray tear and clears her throat. "Now, I'd like to dive into some of these delicious looking goodies. Alina, you really make all of these?"

She looks over at me, and then back at Mom. "I do. Every morning and night, I'm here and do a lot during the day as well. I don't make huge batches of anything, so they don't go bad, and the variety is great. And then, I, of course, do the party type baking on the side."

"When do you have time to have a life?"

Alina presses a hand to her chest and giggles. "I don't necessarily. But I never really feel like I'm missing out. Cam's been nice enough to understand the time requirements of my job and comes to spend the morning and evening shifts with me while I get things ready. And our daily lunch."

Taking her hand in mine, I kiss the back of it. "I'm happy to be here with you. It's always been my favorite place to watch you work."

For a moment, I get lost in Alina's eyes. All the things I want to say and do to her running through my head. But the moment is quickly gone when it's clear Mom is crying.

We both look over at her, and I move to get out of my seat, but she waves me off, digging a tissue out of her purse. "I'm sorry. It's just the one thing I'm sad I won't get to see. That and grandbabies. I always thought I'd be the fun grandma."

I have to clear my throat before I can answer. "You would be, Mom."

A somber silence wraps around us, nobody really sure what to say or how to break the tension that's enveloped us.

"I think I'd like to go home now, dear. This tired me out a bit more than I anticipated."

I'm up off my seat in an instant, reaching my hands out to help Mom out of her chair. "Of course."

Alina stands too, also reaching out to help Mom up. "It was lovely to see you, Barbara. Thank you for coming by today."

Mom wraps Alina in a hug and pulls her close. She whispers something in her ear that causes Alina's gaze to dash over my way, her eyes glassy. Whatever it is, it's depressing as fuck.

When they finally separate, I give Mom my arm and head toward the exit. "I'll see you tonight," I say over my shoulder. My only focus right now is getting Mom home.

I'm happy she was able to come out to see Alina today.

I just hope it's not the last time.

Chapter 17
Alina

"How long?" Cameron's question is urgent as he shakes me to pull me from sleep. I wish I could say it was deep, but unfortunately, tonight's not agreeing with me.

"What? What are you talking about?" I push myself up to sit and clear the grogginess from my throat before I wipe the sand from my eyes.

"The nightmares. How long have you been having nightmares, Alina?"

"I don't know what you're talking about." I start to turn away, but Cameron grips my shoulders and turns me toward him.

Ducking low, he meets my eyes as his fingers dig into the bare skin of my shoulder. Wriggling under his grip, I try to get him to loosen up, but there's fire licking at his irises.

"Ow, Cam, you're hurting me."

"I need to know how long you've been having them." He's absolutely frantic. His eyes are wide and wild, body tense with a slight shudder.

"It's none of your damn business." I've had nightmares from the beginning. They're terrible, awful things where I see my parents dying and can never get to them. It changes all the time, but I'm always stuck where I am watching them slowly die while they scream for help.

"It is. I was here with you when you buried them. I held you while you cried. You were okay. You were doing okay...you were healing."

"And then you left!" I practically shout and cringe at how high my voice sounds.

His head falls forward.

"You left, Cameron. And my whole world fell apart all over again. You were the one thing keeping me together, keeping me whole, keeping me sane. When you left, that all changed." The words rush out of me, laden with pain and heartache.

Without a single utterance, he yanks me into his chest. "You need help, Ali. You need to find somebody to help you work through this. It's been over a decade since they died, and you clearly still haven't dealt with it."

Pushing away, I straighten up. "You don't know what you're talking about."

Taking my wrists in his hands, he pulls me back to him. "Alina, you still can't even say the word '*family*.'"

I shudder at the word.

"That's not being okay."

"What do you want from me? My parents were ripped away from me in a horrific crime one night. One minute they're there, and the next, they're gone. And I was sixteen years old. That's a pretty vulnerable age to lose your parents and have your life turned upside down." The words angrily pour from my mouth, and Cameron's lips press into a firm line.

"And then, the person who I found comfort and solace in, the one person who helped me keep it together, disappeared without a word. Again, the person I relied on was there one moment and gone the next. I literally woke up and called you, only to get a voicemail and never a return call. Do you know what that was like for me?" My eyes narrow as I take in the look of horror on his face. I'm not trying to blame him, but he needs to understand the role he played in all of this.

"So excuse me if I still have nightmares sometimes."

"You need *help*, Alina." He tries to take my hands in his, but I pull away.

"Maybe I don't want any."

"You can't keep living like this. Based on tonight, I know this isn't a once in a while thing." Jumping off the bed, he starts pacing at the end of it, running a hand through his hair.

"How could you know that?" Terror takes over.

We've been lucky this hasn't happened during the past several weeks he's been staying at my house. This is the first nightmare I've had since he started spending the night, probably because I feel safe and secure with him in my bed and wrapped around me. I'm not sure why tonight is different, except for the visit with his mom playing over and over in my mind.

"Because when people have a singular nightmare, they wake up freaked out and worried and often can't get back to sleep. But you basically moved on like it was nothing, despite the fact that you were yelling and screaming and crying." He kneels on the floor in front of me and holds on to my waist.

"Please, Alina. I can't bear the thought of you suffering like this. When we first got back together, I saw how tired you were, and I thought it was just your hours. Now I know better and hate myself for being so stupid, for not thinking more of it. For not pressing or asking." He's pleading with me, and I don't understand why.

If this is suddenly an issue for him, maybe he should have been sure to be around to make sure I was okay. He doesn't get to comment on how I'm coping, or possibly not coping, after so much time away.

"Why do you care so much?"

"Because I love you, Alina. I've always loved you and worried about you and wanted what's best for you." His words only mean so much to me right now.

"Then why'd you stay away for so long? How can you claim to have always loved me if you were gone for so damn long?"

His chin drops to his chest and his head hangs in my lap. "I'm sorry, Ali. I can't apologize enough. Really. I can spend the rest of my life trying to make it up to you and never fully be able to. Because you're right. There's no excuse for such a long absence."

I'm completely frozen, with my hands hovering above Cameron's upper half because I'm not sure if I want to touch him. Because as much as I thought I'd forgiven him and moved on from the hurt of it, now that I'm faced with it again, I'm wondering if that's true.

Am I still hung up on the pain he caused when he left? Have I just fallen back into things with him because he's here again and I've missed him for half my life?

My head is spinning, and I can't tell up from down.

Suddenly, I feel like a teenager again, reeling from the loss of her boyfriend, her first love, maybe her truest love. But have I really gotten over the fact that he was gone?

I accept his reasoning. It makes sense. I hate that he had to struggle through that, and basically alone, but do I forgive him for his absence?

"Alina, talk to me please."

"I'm wondering how I feel right now. This happened so fast. And I thought it was because I never stopped loving you, because I'm pretty sure I haven't, but now I'm wondering if you being back just threw me back to being a teenager and into that part of life again. But we're not those people anymore, Cam. We're adults now. And I feel like we don't know each other that well."

"What do you want to know? I'm an open book." He speaks calmly, but there's a look of panic in his eyes. Desperation.

"Tell me more about your addiction. How you manage it day-to-day. How can I be confident you won't relapse and leave me again?"

He lifts his head and locks his eyes on me. "Even if I relapse, I will *never* leave you again, Alina. That was the hardest thing I've ever done, harder than getting clean. Harder than coming back, which trust me, was no easy thing. But I've been clean for ten years now and have learned how to cope. Like going to the gym, which I do somewhat regularly when back home. I stay away from other substances, like alcohol. And I have a kick ass sponsor named Spencer, who I'd love for you to meet."

When I say nothing, he rises and scoots onto the bed, lying back in his spot and pulling me to rest against his chest. He starts twirling curls between his fingers and running his fingertips up and down my forearm.

"It all started from an injury, and then I liked the feeling of numbness and nothingness the pain relievers brought me. So, I avoid that feeling now. I may have *a* drink here and there, but I limit it to one. If I ever am hurt, I try to power through, depending on how bad it is. If it's really bad, I opt for over-the-counter stuff. My doctor wanted to give me a muscle relaxer for my back once and I said no. It's about self-control. I try to have it, and so far, I haven't failed."

While ten years' worth of being drug free is an astounding feat, and one I'm proud of him for, I worry that he hasn't encountered any truly difficult times yet. Times when he'd want to disappear again.

"I'm nervous about when your mom dies." My voice is so meek and quiet. The only indication that he even heard me is the fact that his whole body tenses.

"I'm worried about that too because I feel like the desire and pull will be strong. But I'm hoping I'll have you on my side and in my corner, and as somebody I can turn to, to help me cope. Spencer is fully aware of what I'm doing here and made sure I knew he was only a call away and would even come out here if I needed him to. It's a scary situation, and I'm thinking about it already, but I'm trying to prep myself so I can be strong."

"I'll be here with you." I loop my arm around his waist and squeeze. I can't imagine being anywhere else because I *do* love Cameron. Yes, part of it may be the Cameron he used to be, but in so many ways, he's still the same person.

I think there are things about people that change over time, and some that stay the same. Because the type of person you are is likely the type of person you'll always be. Yes, Cameron may be an addict, which worries me, but he tries to have control of that. But the person he is beyond that; kind, caring, always putting me first, those things haven't changed. He shows me that he loves me on a daily basis by sitting, likely bored out of his mind, watching me prep. Not just once a day, but twice.

"It takes a lot of talking, going through the feelings and how getting high isn't a better option. But I have a good support system."

"Do you have friends too?"

"A few, of course. But only one or two who are addicts too who would get it. And sometimes you don't want to rope them into your problems. I'm confident that with you and Spencer, I'll be okay. It'll be a real test, though." He sounds nervous as he talks about it, a slight waver to his voice that gives away the unsureness he's feeling.

"I still feel like we don't know each other that much. We had ten years go by without each other. There are things about me you don't know and things I experienced."

"So tell me, Ali. I want to know everything. Even the other men you dated and the one you almost married."

"I didn't almost marry him. That's an exaggeration. I broke up with him when I found out he was going to propose. And a big reason was because he wasn't you." I tilt my head up to meet Cam's eyes. And I find nothing but desire swirling through them. "I don't want to talk anymore."

He runs a hand along my jaw and grips my chin, closing his mouth over mine. With just the right amount of pressure, he eases my lips apart and his tongue slides in to swirl along mine.

His fingertips glide down my arm and to my abdomen, sliding under the hem of my tank top. A chill runs through me as my skin pebbles from the lightest of touches, and I sigh into his mouth.

His lips become more forceful against mine, and he shifts us so I'm on my back and he's resting on his side, his hand gliding up to cup my breast. With a gentle but skilled hand, he massages before taking my nipple between his fingers and tweaking it. My back arches as I try to get closer to his hand, wanting and needing more.

But instead of giving in to my request, his fingers dance down my body and trail along my panties. He pushes them to the side and runs one finger along my soaking pussy, teasing me as he inserts the tip just a bit before swirling around my clit.

Just as I'm about to pull away and beg for more, he plunges two fingers inside me and moves them deftly. My mouth gasps away from his as my back arches and my nails dig into his shoulders.

The more he moves his fingers inside me, the more my legs fall apart. He shifts and lowers his face to my chest, pulling my nipple into his mouth through the silky fabric of my tank top. Despite the garment being in the way, I can feel the warmth of his breath, the wetness of his mouth, and the pressure of his tongue.

I grip harder at his shoulders as my hips start to buck against his hand, needing more. "Faster, Cam."

With no more than a groan against my chest, he adds another finger, causing me to cry out as he pumps them into me feverishly. He hooks them, making me writhe and tip to the side as my arm wraps around his head to hold him close as I start to tremble.

I'm standing on the precipice, ready to fall, when he bites down on my nipple, sending a trill straight through me, and I scream his name and fall into oblivion.

He slows his fingers and moves his face to be level with mine.

"I haven't forgotten how to make you come, Ali. And I certainly haven't forgotten what you sound like when you do. It's a sound that used to haunt my dreams, and I've longed for it to fill my ears for a decade."

With a whimper, my hand dives into his pants and grips him hard, to which he groans and tips his head back.

"Show me. Show how well you know my body and can make me come." I pull my fist up his shaft and his fingers flutter against my stomach.

Quickly, he tears off my panties and his pants, lowering himself over me. I love watching the way his muscles ripple as he uses them to hold himself above me. Being underneath Cam is one of my favorite places to be.

He uses the tip of his cock to tease me, slipping it along my soaked entrance but not penetrating me. He swirls around my clit before descending and plunging into me. My head tips back with a moan and my hands grip at his shoulders, nails scratching down his biceps.

"It's so good, Cam."

"Fuck, Ali. You're perfect. You take my cock like such a good girl."

"You're the only one who could ever make me feel this good."

His head falls to my chest with a groan before he pushes himself up straight and starts thrusting into me hard and fast. Every pump inside me has me wanting and needing more and more. It's like he knows as I match his thrusts and buck toward him with every one, and he drives into me with reckless abandon.

Before long, sweat begins to bead on his skin, and I lean up and lick the trail along his neck. In response, he bends and latches his teeth onto my collarbone, causing me to scream his name as I clench down and hold him tightly, deep inside my pussy, while he groans and his dick pulsates.

"Oh, God, Alina. You're so fucking perfect."

Every time he says that I want to shrink into myself. I'm far from perfect. In fact, this whole thing started because of my nightmares. That's not perfection.

I forcefully roll away from him. "You didn't seem to think I was perfect an hour ago."

He grabs my cheeks firmly between his hands and turns me to him, our faces so close his nose almost brushes mine. "I am *worried* about you, Alina. That's not thinking you aren't perfection in a five-foot-four package with chocolate curls and caramel eyes. It's realizing that there's something bigger going on here and being concerned for you and your well-being."

I try to shake out of his grasp, but it only makes him hold tighter.

"I love you, and I care about you. I am going to be here to make sure that you're okay. Even if it's the last thing I ever do."

While everything in me wants to believe him, the more we've gotten into this, the harder it's been to see past him leaving. It all feels too much the same. The nightmares are mostly gone when he's wrapped around me. We spend any and all free time together. We love each other.

It all feels just a little too familiar, and I can't help the thoughts and sensations that I'm just waiting for the rest to fall into place too.

And what that means is that he leaves me again. And this time, I'm not sure I'd survive it.

Chapter 18

Cameron

I can't believe she's still having nightmares. How could I be so blind? Have I just been in a haze of loving her again that I can't see the negatives? It's a glaring sign to miss.

All it does is point out how much Alina is *not* confiding in me. Which means she doesn't trust me. Not that I can blame her there. I shattered her trust, and she may only now be picking up the billions of pieces of that I left behind. I have to help her, be the glue that puts it back together.

The problem is, I have no idea how to do that.

I'm here, physically, mentally and emotionally, and it doesn't seem to be enough.

She didn't even really answer my question about the frequency of them. Sure, I've been staying with her for weeks now and it hadn't happened yet, but even once a month is far too many.

That means I can only do one thing. If I'm not going to get answers from the source herself, I have to go to the next best thing. The source's closest confidante.

I get to the bakery early on Tuesday, hoping Alina will still be in the kitchen working on whatever delicious concoction she has planned next.

"Hey. Alina should be out any minute." Liv's become far more pleasant in recent weeks, and now her pregnancy is officially showing. When Alina told me she was pregnant, I had a brief moment of panic that Ali was going to start getting baby fever, but then I realize that Alina not only isn't that sort of person, but that even if she was, I'd happily have children with her at any point in the near or far future.

Shock had been another feeling, partially because Liv is the baby and still only twenty-four, but also because she just got married.

She and Jameson both accepted my heartfelt congratulations, and Liv even gave me a hug, so I'm hoping she'll talk to me now. And honestly.

"Liv." It must be the tone in my voice because she stops wiping the counter and looks at me.

"Yes?"

"How long has Alina been having nightmares?"

Her mouth parts into a perfect 'O' and her eyes widen to the size of saucers. The look is gone just as quickly, though, as she shakes it away and clears her throat. "I don't know what you're talking about."

Ah. So we're going to make this difficult.

"I know that's bullshit, Liv."

Her hand finds her stomach. "It's not. And it's really something you should talk to Alina about." She turns away and bends down to rearrange the neat and tidy bakery display case.

I round the corner of the counter and gently take her bicep in my hand, pulling her up and turning her to me. "Liv. We have the same goal. I'm worried about Alina."

Her shoulders slump, and I know without her having to say anything I'm on the right track and that Liv feels the same way.

"I need to know how long they've been happening. And how frequently."

"It's not an answer you're going to like. It's going to hurt." There's something to her tone that I can't place but it almost seems like concern. For me.

"I can take it. This is for Alina." It doesn't matter what she tells me. The only thing that matters here is Alina's well-being.

"Years, Cam. Basically since you left. She goes through bouts. Sometimes they're only once a month, but sometimes it's every day."

The words slice through me like a knife through butter, stealing all my air. I can't believe she held this in.

"We used to live together so I could help her easily. When we got our own places, she'd stay with me a lot when they were bad. But then she started calling and I'd go over to her. Honestly, with how much you've been together, I'm surprised this hasn't come up sooner."

"She just had her first one the other night." My own voice sounds so far away.

Liv crosses her arms against her chest and sighs. "That's a good thing, Cam. It's been, what, three months? More? And you're with her every night. That's a better track record than she's ever had."

"They had stopped before...before..."

"Before you left?" She doesn't say it with any accusation or anger. She says it with genuine curiosity.

"Yeah."

"But you did. And Alina fell apart all over again. It was hard to watch, Cam. There's a reason we hated you, a reason I was hard on you, and why Mazie and Eli basically haven't been by. For years, you were an honorary Baker, but after you left...we were the ones here to pick up the pieces of

Alina. It was hard on all of us because we were all still grieving our own losses."

This is the most honest Liv's ever been with me. And all too soon I see that I've been wrong to still think about her as the baby Baker and not the full-grown adult that she is.

"I know. I know! But there has to be something to do about it now. Something to make her better."

Liv rests her hand on mine. "Cam, I'm not sure there's anything that will ever make any of us truly better. While I agree that Alina needs help with the nightmares, we'll never be healed. We'll never be whole again. We're just learning how to go on with life without our parents here for the big moments. And I'm getting a firsthand experience with that, and as the baby, I'm going first." She runs her hand over her stomach again as she looks up at the ceiling.

My heart aches for her. She's the first to get married, to have a baby, and she's doing it all without her parents and without her older siblings' guidance on how to get through it. She's the one paving the way for everybody else, which can't be easy being the youngest.

"How do we convince her to get help with the nightmares, at least? To talk to somebody. I begged and pleaded when everything first happened. I thought it'd be a great idea for all of you, but she didn't want to hear of it, and I didn't want to push, and then I had to leave for rehab." I'm not sure what Alina has told Liv, but I'm sure it's enough. Even if it's not, there's nothing to hide from this family. Especially if I hope to be part of it someday, which I do.

She doesn't skip a beat, so she's either hiding her surprise well, or Alina told them. Or at least Liv.

"I was hoping it wouldn't come to that since she hasn't called me in a few months. Or that you had helped her through it. But I don't know.

I've been begging for *years*, Cam. And not just for my own mental sanity and sleep. She won't listen to me. Mazie and Eli have no idea the severity of it, and that could be my fault for listening to her wishes and keeping it quieter around them, but what was I supposed to do?"

Her eyes turn glassy, and I pull her into a hug. "It's okay. We'll figure it out together. But it may be a good idea to get the older siblings involved too. I know they know it was happening at one point, since you all lived together at home. You have to tell them the nightmares came back and have been for some time."

She grumbles but nods before pulling away. It's been ten years, but I still look at Liv as my little sister, and I'd do anything to protect her. I know she's scared of the reaction her siblings are going to have about not having been informed of the sleep issues Alina exhibits, but they'll all bond and come together for Alina. I'm sure of it.

"Hey, Cam." Her sweet voice fills my ears, and I know immediately this conversation with Liv is over, even before she turns away from me and busies herself making coffees.

"Hey, Ali. I was a little early so Liv and I were just chatting while you finished up."

"Oh yeah? What were you talking about?" There's a wide smile on her face of genuine curiosity.

"Nothing important." Liv makes direct eye contact with me while handing me my cup. She doesn't want to put Alina in a bad mood or on the defensive, and I can't say I blame her.

"Just...random things." If she senses anything amiss or has any qualms about us talking, she doesn't show it as she walks over to our usual table.

It's not that I want to be secretive around Alina, or that I don't want her to know what Liv and I were talking about. But I trust Liv's judgment, and if she thinks that we shouldn't be straightforward just yet, then I agree.

Besides, the way Alina shut down and got defensive the other night, it took me a full day to build things back up to how they had been. Whatever walls Alina erected around herself when I left, she slowly started to dismantle when I came back and proved to her I'm here to stay. Those immediately went back up when I questioned her nightmare.

The next morning, she was distant, far from lovey dovey, and barely made eye contact while we ate the breakfast she made. It took me nuzzling her neck and telling her how much I love her to get back to semi-solid ground.

At the moment, I feel like I'm walking on eggshells, trying not to say the wrong thing because I don't want those walls going back up. I don't want her to feel like she has to be defensive around me, when all I'm trying to do is protect her and help her.

It's a fine line, and I'm not sure I'm walking straight.

Chapter 19
Alina

C am has been different since my nightmare. Thankfully, I haven't
had another since, but one was more than enough to change our
dynamic. I can tell he doesn't really know what to do or say or how to
act without thinking I'm going to have a meltdown again.

In reality, he should just not bring it up again. Ever.

I'm fine. I'll *be* fine. The nightmares have been better now that Cam's
back. Just one in a few months is amazing. Way better than I'd been doing
before, and I'm sure Liv is just as excited about it as I am. Especially since
she's pregnant and needs her sleep.

It's not until I walk out of the kitchen for the first time in the morning
that I realize something's amiss. Mazie and Eli are both here. They're
almost never here at the same time, especially Eli.

While he invested some of his money into the business, he chose to
be a silent partner, not even wanting his name on any of the paperwork.
We turn to him with any big questions or concerns if they come up, like
when we talked about expanding a few years ago, but that's about it.

I'm hesitant as I slow my pace. They were clearly talking about something they don't want me hearing, as they've completely stopped and all planted their fake smiles on their faces.

"Hey, guys. Maze, Eli, glad you're here today." I give a round of hugs, even to Liv, though I've seen her at least ten times this morning alone.

Whatever this is, it was planned, because this is our morning lull when I tend to come out and get some things organized and talk to Liv about upcoming ideas or what she'd like for the afternoon.

There's hesitation in my tone, my actions. What are they doing here? And why the secrecy? Sure, I'm not always up on when they'll be here, but this seems like more than just a friendly visit from the atmosphere in the room.

It's then I notice the sign has been turned to *Closed*. Something's definitely going on here.

Panic wraps around my ribs, squeezing so I can barely get a breath. Cam. Where's Cam? Did he leave again? Did he tell them he was going to and asked them to be here to lighten the load? To help cushion the fall?

Because it won't help.

"Alina, breathe." Mazie's voice in my ear stops the whooshing but doesn't slow the rapid breaths or racing heart.

"What's going on? Why are you all here in the middle of the day?"

"Can't we come see you to say hi?" Eli likes to pretend nothing is going on, that this is the most normal thing in the world, but he knows it's not, and I can tell by the way he runs a hand up the back of his head.

"Somebody tell me what's going on before I go into full-blown panic mode. Where's Cam? What happened to Cam? Did he leave again?"

"I asked him not to come today." Finally, Liv speaks. She's been extra quiet and won't meet my eyes. Why do I have a feeling she has something to do with this? Whatever *this* is.

"Not to come to what? It's like this is some sort of intervention or something with the way you're all acting."

And when they all make eye contact with each other, that's when I realize this is exactly what it is. They're here for some sort of intervention. For me. Is it Cam? Are they really that against him?

"Mazie, Eli, I know you guys hate Cam, but this feels a little extreme. And Liv, I thought you were on my side. I thought you'd come around to Cam."

"It's not about Cam, Leen. This is about *you*." Mazie runs a hand down my back. What could possibly be about me?

And then it all dawns on me, and my eyes lock on Olivia, who quickly looks away as guilt shrouds her face.

"How could you?" There's a mix of hurt and anger in my voice and my chest.

"Don't blame this on Olivia." Eli's quick to come to the defense of Liv any time. Sometimes, I think it's because she's the baby. Sometimes I think it's because she's his favorite. "You should have come to us yourself, Alina. How could you not tell me or Mazie that you're still having nightmares? We thought they passed long ago."

"And not only that you've been having them, but the frequency too."

My pulse reverberates through my ears as my chest heaves.

"Liv. How could you betray me like this? You're supposed to be my best friend and my sister." She shrinks away from my angry words, a hand flying to her stomach.

"I'm also your sister, and Eli is your brother, and we had no idea because you chose to keep it a secret and begged Liv to do the same.

Which is a problem in and of itself, but one we can get over. The problem here, Alina, is that you need help." Mazie's tone has taken on the one I've always associated with Mom. It's almost as if she practiced sounding like her.

"I'm fine. I don't know why Liv bothered you with this." I huff, swallowing the lump in my throat.

"Because I asked her to." At the sound of Cameron's voice, I spin around. He's standing by the door with his hands firmly in his pockets, guilt strewn across his face, concern lacing his eyes.

"Why would you do that? You went behind my back to talk to her? Don't you think that's maybe not the best idea for you to be doing, as we're working on getting things back?"

"Here's the thing, Ali. I don't care. I don't care if it upsets you. I don't care that we went behind your back. Because I'm worried about you, and so is your sister. Enough so that she was able to override the guilt she felt even talking to Eli and Mazie." At the mention of their names, they both look over at Cam, tense as a statue. This is the first they've been in the same room in a decade.

I'm pretty sure the only reason Eli isn't going for the jugular right now is because that's not what this is about. In fact, Cam put all of this together because of his concern for me. That has to score him some major points with the big siblings.

"You need help, Ali. Help we can't give you." At this, he opens his arms wide and gestures toward my siblings.

"I'm *fine*."

"You're not, LeeLee. And it's all but killed me to keep your secret. I couldn't do it anymore. I had to tell them so you could get the help you need. There's no shame in talking to somebody, Alina. In seeking out help." Liv turns to me with tears in her eyes, and I know they'd be there even without her pregnancy hormones.

She's been begging me for years and never had somebody to back her up and was too loyal to go to Eli and Mazie without my say so.

Cam changed that. And while I want to be mad at them all, I can't be. Because I'm exhausted. Mentally and physically. It's not until recently that I've had even remotely decent sleep, and that's with Cam being back.

What if he leaves again? I need to be able to cope without him.

This revelation causes me to soften. It's not so much I've never thought about seeking help, but I've been scared to. Now, at least I know that I have my siblings and my boyfriend all backing me up and are here to support me.

"You're right. All of you. I do need help. I just don't know how to find it." I drop my chin to my chest in shame, but fingers lace with my own on both hands, and I look up to find Cam on one side and Eli on the other. While holding my hands, they shake and nod at each other and somehow it seems like everything that went on between us, all the bad blood, is in the past.

And if it's not for Eli, I'll make sure it is. Because Cam is here for me, he's being here for me, he's doing something I haven't been able to do for myself in years. And he's not taking no for an answer.

"I'll help you, Ali. We all will. It's about finding a therapist and speaking to them regularly and diving deep."

"I've been scared about your judgment if I sought therapy." I speak to the floor instead of my siblings. But when silence fills the café, I look up and find their faces filled with remorse and more concern.

"Leen, I see a therapist every other week."

Mazie is in therapy? I had no idea. It's surprising some of the things we keep close to the vest.

"Eli did after he dropped out of MIT. Liv did right after it happened. We told you, there was no shame then, but you were young and didn't want to. We didn't feel like we could force it. Maybe that was a mistake on our part and we should have. But this is a huge thing to have happened to us and at vulnerable ages. We *all* should be or should have at one point, seen somebody about it."

"I see a therapist too, Ali. In addition to having a sponsor and going to meetings when I need one or just haven't been in a while. Which, I'd really like you to join me at a meeting, if that's okay with you. I think seeing what we talk about, what we go through, may be beneficial for you."

"I'm not an addict, though. Isn't that frowned upon?"

"There are some sessions where friends and family members are encouraged to come. I'll ask Spencer when one is coming up if you'd like to join me. And even with you not being an addict, you can learn a lot. There's a million reasons people use; some you might not find to be much different from what you're going through." He pulls my hand to his mouth and kisses my knuckles.

"Yes. I think I'd like to come to that." It'd be nice to learn a little bit about Cam and what his process looks like. I know it's different for everybody, but having a little glimpse into it might make me feel better. It's a level of intimacy and way of knowing Cam that I'd like to have.

The thought of going to therapy still scares me. Not just because I have to be vulnerable in a way I never have been, but because I have to go through and relive all the terribleness that brought me to this point in the first place.

I often wonder how my siblings are so composed all the time, how they can go through life not worrying about things and reliving things the way

I do. But at the same time, I have something to keep me hyper-fixated on it that they don't. And it's something I've never shared with any of them.

Though maybe it's time that demon I keep to myself came out into the open.

Chapter 20

Cameron

A weight has been lifted from my chest since Alina agreed to see a therapist. Of course, Mazie came in clutch with a page filled with recommendations of local to semi-local practitioners who would be good for Alina to contact. Not just names and numbers but important details like what they specialize in as well.

I sat next to her that night while she looked through the list, trying to decide who she felt would be best to call and who she felt she may be able to save time and not bother with.

So far, she's decided she'd prefer a female who practices outside of Juniper Grove. I can't blame her there. It's such a small town, and while doctor-patient confidentiality is real, so is the small-town rumor mill.

All it would take is one visit for her to be seen by the wrong person for the rumors to start flying.

While she doesn't seem to feel like there's anything wrong with seeking therapy, not anymore at least, she doesn't want everybody to know that she is. I can understand wanting that privacy. It's more that people are going to ask questions that she maybe doesn't want to answer. They'll harp on the fact that it's about the deaths of her parents and she'll have to deal with that over and over, on top of digging deep about it in therapy.

She's in for a long and probably difficult road. It's not easy to sit and talk about your innermost turmoil on a weekly basis. But I'm here for her every step of the way. I'm sure at some point she'll dive into my leaving, my absence, and then, of course, my reappearance in her life. And that likely won't be easy on us. But I'm not going anywhere this time.

As more time passes, Alina becomes more frantic about the whole process, asking questions about things that aren't a big deal.

"How do I find the time? There's so much to do at the café."

"You make time, Alina. And there's plenty of it in the day. Your hours are over the top anyway, so you take two hours to go to therapy."

"What if I don't like my therapist?" She's chewing on her cuticles in between questions, and I have to keep pulling her hand away from her mouth.

"Then you find a new one." I squeeze her fingers in mine. "Trust me, Alina. All will be well. And you'll feel bad sometimes, and that's okay. You can confide in me about anything you talked about that you need to work out, or you can talk to your siblings, or you can process it alone. But we're all here for you."

"I don't know why I'm getting so worked up about this. It's just...opening myself up like that? I've spent so long doing the opposite." She stares at her folded legs on the couch.

"I know. And I'd love to tell you it's easy, but I'm not going to lie to you. There will be good days and bad days too. But I'm here with you, for all of it."

Her fingers pick idly at the hem of her pants. "What if it causes issues between us? I'm going to have to go into how you left again. I know we're back together, but I also know, deep down, there are feelings I never truly processed about that."

With one finger, I tip her chin up so those gorgeous caramel eyes can meet mine. "Hey. We'll get through it. If you want to. I meant what I said, Ali. I'm here. And if you want me to leave, well, I'll fight like hell not to, but if it's what you really want, I won't argue with you on it. I know that I left without a word and that's a hell of a thing to get over and absorb, and I'd understand if you realized you'd never really be able to forgive me for it."

"I don't know that I feel that way...I hope I don't. You've been here and proven you want to be here and with me. Your mom is dying, and you spend more time with me than her."

My jaw ticks at this statement. It's an avoidance tactic, and I'm not sure Alina sees it as such. If I avoid seeing Mom, being around her, and in her presence, in my mind, it's easier to deny that she's dying. Because now I can see it clear as day on her face. The doctors are surprised she's lasted this long, but I can tell it won't be much longer.

That's the time I'm most scared for. I know I can handle Alina's emotions and concerns. I can handle her doubts in me and the relationship and make her understand that I'm *here* and I'm here for her. But when Mom passes, I'm not sure how to handle that. It's going to be hard, and the call back to the numbness of the pills is going to be strong. It already has been at times when Mom was rushed to the hospital.

She's had a few close calls in recent years, but nothing like this. Nothing has been this bad, this severe, this final. The doctors basically gave her a death sentence, and now we're just waiting for it to come to pass.

The waiting is the worst part. Every day I know I have less and less time with her, yet I can't bring myself to spend it with her because I'm afraid of it ending. It's a horrible circle to be caught in.

But in the end, the one person who's going to understand what it's like to lose a parent, what the world feels like without them, is Alina. Because she's lost both and when she was much younger than I am. Yes, the circumstances are vastly different, but the loss of a parent is still a great loss. One that age doesn't have any effect on.

When you're older, and your parent is older, you hope they go peacefully but know they lived a full life. When they're sick, like Mom, you hope they don't suffer for too long. That's the only solace I find. Mom is suffering. She'd never say so and never let anybody know that she's in pain or uncomfortable, but I know she is.

It's in her stilted movements, and the light in her eyes is long gone. Though she tries to keep them subtle, she moans and groans more in the little movements she makes throughout the day. It's even how much more help she's asking for lately.

And I'm a coward hiding out with my girlfriend instead of facing it head on. No wonder Alina doesn't think I'll be able to handle it when the time comes. I can barely handle it now.

While she's not wrong, it's going to be hard, I'm *not* going to relapse. I refuse to. And I know with her help, I won't.

Chapter 21
Alina

I start with my new therapist in a week. To say I'm nervous would be the understatement of the century. It's been a long time trying to bury the thoughts and feelings and things that cause the nightmares. And to dive back into that, well, it's not exactly at the top of my list of most wanted things to do.

It's been causing me fitful nights of sleep and far more nightmares. Probably because it's in the forefront of my mind.

Tonight has been no different, though I'm not woken by a nightmare. When I wake, it's slow, as something buzzing pulls me from sleep.

It's then I realize it's Cam's cell phone and my heart stops. There's only one reason he'd get a call in the middle of the night like this.

A quick glance at the clock tells me it's two in the morning. The sky is still sprinkled with stars, and the moonlight shines through my gauzy curtains, casting a light over Cam that makes him look angelic.

He must not hear it, because he doesn't wake up.

Gently, I shake his shoulder. "Cam." He doesn't move. So I jostle him a little harder. "Cam, baby. Wake up."

He groans and stretches, but it's too late. The call stopped. "What? Did I sleep through a nightmare?" He sounds incredulous, and I know it's because he's not sure he could. Though I've woken him up once when it wasn't a screaming nightmare so much as just waking up with a jolt and crying hysterically.

"No, your phone was—" I'm cut off by it buzzing again.

He jolts upright, the blanket pooling around hips as he grabs it off the nightstand and swipes. "Hello?"

Even though he's under the moonlight, he looks exceptionally pale.

Without words, his forehead drops into his palm and the phone slips from his hand. The screen is already dark, and I move it from the blanket, climbing into his lap and putting my arms over his shoulders.

His arms loop around my waist, and his head finds the crook of my neck. Then the dam breaks, and his body starts to shake as he cries.

I squeeze him tightly, losing a hand in his hair and kissing his temple. "It's okay, Cam. Let it out. I'm right here." There's a sting behind my eyes as they start to fill, and I glance up at the ceiling to will the sensation away.

I loved his mom, and while it's acceptable to cry with him, for him, for her and the loss, now is not the time. I need to be strong for him, be his pillar of support like he was for me all those years ago.

He holds me so tightly, I can barely breathe, but it's worth it to be this close to him and be a true comfort for him in his time of need.

The tears don't last long, though. Cam's never been much of a crier or an overly emotional person. When he lifts his head, his eyelashes are matted down and wet, and he looks so young, so much like the child who left me and less like the adult who came back for me.

"Dad said she went peacefully. That she was there one minute and just gone the next. I guess she'd been sleeping, and the monitors started going off."

"I'm so sorry, Cam."

His hands push into his hair, and he pulls at the roots. "I should have been there. I should have been by her side."

I wrap my fingers around his wrists and lower them, placing them in my lap. "There's no way you could have known tonight would be the night. Besides, you'd have been sleeping in your own room. It's two in the morning, Cam. You wouldn't have been by her side anyway." I run my own fingers through his blond locks and brush my hand down his stubbled cheek.

His chest rises and falls with a heavy sigh. "You're right. I know you're right. But I still feel like I should have been there."

"I get it. It's a feeling I understand. I felt like I should have been with my parents. Not that I would have been able to stop the carjacking but, I don't know, maybe I would have been able to point out the person or something."

"Alina, you know—"

I press my lips to his to cut him off. "I know I couldn't have prevented it. I do. It's just one of those feelings that you have. But know that it's the same for you. You would have been sleeping. There's no way you would have known tonight was the night."

"It's going to be so weird going back to that house without her."

"Do you want me to go with you?" Taking his hand in mine, I kiss his palm.

"I don't know. I do, but I don't know how Dad will take it. Part of me feels like it should be just us, but at the same time, I want you there, need you there."

"Maybe you deserve to be a little selfish. If it's what you need, if you think it will help you in the long run." I don't want to be too specific, but I hope he knows what I'm alluding to. It's not that I don't trust Cam, but this is a hard situation, and he might be quick to turn back to his old habits of numbing his emotions. "But if you feel like you need to be alone with your dad, I understand that too. Just know I'm here."

"I do." He sighs heavily and shakes his head. "I guess I'm done sleeping for tonight." Straightening his legs, he supports me as my ass hits the bed.

I shift to move off his lap, but he tightens his grip around my waist, pulling me closer to him. "Not yet. Just...don't get up yet."

Instead of shifting off the bed, I rest my head against his bare chest, hearing his heart pick up in tempo at our connection.

I wish I knew more of what to do for him, say to him. But this situation, while still the loss of a parent, is so different from what I went through. Not only are we full-fledged adults now, but this wasn't sudden. It was a long time coming and expected. Does that make it different?

Loss is still loss, I suppose. The only difference is that as an adult, Cameron has more tools to help deal with his emotions. I hope.

Chapter 22

Cameron

Nothing's the same. While I knew this was coming, nothing truly prepared me for it.

Mom's been gone for a week, and I've still barely come to terms with it. Every time I swing by the house, I still expect her to come out of the kitchen or down the hall from her bedroom with a giant smile on her face, even though she hasn't been like that for months.

The funeral was bleak and depressing, which isn't exactly a shock.

Thank God for Alina. She's been my rock, coming with me anywhere I ask her to, keeping her fingers laced through mine the whole time. It can't be easy for her to relive the emotions of a loss, especially that of a parent, but she's been a trooper through the whole thing.

I'm probably the only person who knows she's struggling. It's minor things, like the way her jaw ticks, the way she'll squeeze my hand a little tighter, the slight waver in her voice, or the glassiness of her eyes.

Her siblings all came to the funeral, rallying around us and staying close by the whole time. They moved as a unit, including Jameson and Zachary. It wasn't until the receiving line, when I begged Alina to be in with me, that she broke down as Liv hugged her. I know it was Liv because that's who she's closest to. The sibling bond between the four of them might be like nothing I've ever seen or experienced, but she and Liv are thicker than thieves, stronger than blood. They're sisters *and* best friends.

Liv hugged her tightly, despite her large belly, and the other siblings wrapped around them. When they separated, I pulled Alina into my side and kissed the top of her head. I needed her to know that in that moment, it was okay for her to cry. She'd been a pillar of support up to then, and I didn't want her feeling bad about breaking down.

Besides, I know Alina loved Mom, and Mom loved her right back. Though she'll never get to see us together for the long haul, I'm glad Mom gave us her blessing a few weeks ago. It's something that I didn't realize I wanted or even needed, but now that she's gone, her words ring in my mind. It brings me a sense of peace, of comfort, that I'm with Alina and Mom approved of her.

Because I truly hope Alina is my forever. I don't ever want to wonder what Mom would have thought of somebody I'm dating.

The hardest part is going through Mom's things. Dad has been beside himself and can't bring himself to do it, so it falls to me. There's no rush, as Dad doesn't need to vacate the house, but I think it's important for him to not have all of her things everywhere.

It's just another place Alina's been incredibly crucial.

At the moment, we're surrounded by piles of clothes. I swear the woman wore the same four sweaters and shirts all year. How could she possibly have so many clothes?

"If there's anything you like or think your sisters would like, feel free to take it for them."

"That's generous of you, but I don't think we have the same style."
As she says this with a smile, she holds up a sweater with a cat on it.
Definitely not the same style as Alina or her sisters. "But donating it all
is good. Somebody will find a use for the clothes."

"You'll have to help me when we get to the jewelry. I don't know
what's important or real or anything about it."

"Think your dad wants to keep the wedding rings?"

"Even if he doesn't, I think he should. At least for now. I may have
him look through and see if there's anything else he bought her that he
wants. And same goes with the jewelry, so take anything you like." I wave
my hand in the general direction of the giant jewelry box that houses
the countless earrings, necklaces, bracelets, and rings that always adorned
Mom's body.

"Again, very generous of you. But I'd feel weird taking her jewelry
without her permission."

"Nonsense. She'd want you to have it." I don't need her to have told
me; I know that Mom would be happy for Alina to take any of her earthly
possessions.

"Well, I'll keep that in mind when we go through it." She plants her
hands on her hips and looks around at the various piles. We've tried to
separate things into types of clothing and even things that should be
thrown in the garbage based on wear. Anything with holes ended up in
the toss pile. "You know, we don't have to get it all done today."

"I know. I just want to make life as easy as possible for Dad. He's clearly
struggling." I haven't seen him outside of his workshop in three days. I'm
pretty sure he even sleeps in there.

To be more helpful, I started sleeping here, and Alina was kind enough
to volunteer to join me. Though we've had to squeeze into a full bed, it's
been kind of nice keeping her close all night. Despite a queen-size not

being much larger, we manage to drift more throughout the night. Here, we can't help but stay pressed against one another.

Having her so close has been helpful. I'd like to say I haven't thought about the numbness the pills used to bring, but I'd be a liar.

I sigh heavily as I look around.

"Everything okay?" Alina hooks her arms around mine as she sidles up to me.

"For some reason, I didn't expect it to hurt so much." The pain in my heart hasn't ceased, hasn't lessened. It's like each day goes on as it just pangs as a constant reminder that she's gone. As though I needed another one than her absence.

Alina rests her hand over my heart, knowing exactly where the pain is. I link my fingers through hers and press her palm into my chest.

"How are you handling the pain?" she asks softly.

"Leaning into you."

"That's it, though? Any thoughts?" She doesn't have to elaborate for me to know what she's asking me. Though she's never come right out to talk about my addiction, I know she worries about it, and I can't blame her.

"I'm doing alright for now. While you were in the shower this morning, I called Spencer just for a reminder of why it's not worth it."

"I wish you would have talked to me." Disappointment rings in her tone.

"Of course, I'll talk to you, Ali. It's just...I don't want to scare you away. This is hard and a lot to deal with. Spencer's been there through the lowest of lows. And for a long time. He knows what it's like firsthand."

"Well, I kind of have firsthand knowledge and feelings of losing a parent."

I drop my chin to my chest, breathing out a weighted sigh. "I know. I'm sorry. I'm fucking this up."

"You're not. Just know that I'm here and you can talk to me. You're not going to scare me away."

While her tone is filled with confidence, I really hope that's true. Because I surely wouldn't be able to handle losing Alina after the loss of Mom. If ever.

Chapter 23
Alina

The day I've been dreading is finally here. My first therapy appointment. Though I don't know what to expect, I've been bouncing on my toes since I woke up this morning. And my wake-up call was a nightmare at four in the morning instead of my usual five-thirty.

Of course I've poured as much nervous energy as I can into the kitchen and baking and creating new desserts. Today I tried a caramel chocolate croissant that was really just an ooey gooey mess. It happens now and again, and mostly when I'm anxious, that I really try to focus my brain on creating something new.

I keep glancing at the clock on the stove, hoping it's going to change more than the few minutes it does every time I look. How could only three minutes have passed? It feels like an eternity.

When Cam comes through the door, I nearly jump out of my skin. He pauses, hand still on the door. "You okay?"

"No. But I'm as prepared as I can be."

"Well, I guess that's all that can be expected. Come on, it's time to go." He graciously offered to drive me to my appointment in Pineville City.

I'm sure he knows I'd be a mess behind the wheel, but I have a feeling it's to ensure that I actually get there and don't chicken out.

I follow him out of the kitchen, grabbing my purse on the way. Before we leave the counter, I stop by a very pregnant Liv. She's due within the next few weeks. We have Brittany here today to help out. We've needed to have our employees here a lot more recently with me spending time with Cam and Liv being so pregnant.

Jameson refuses to let her be alone in the café, and I think it's a good idea. She tries to do too much and doesn't respect her limitations. Just a week ago, I caught her climbing on a chair in the stockroom to bring down a box of cups. Sure, the box was light enough, but she shouldn't have been up there in the first place.

"You sure you're okay with me leaving?" I'm almost begging her to say no, that she needs me here, that she's having contractions. Anything.

Instead, she rolls her eyes at me and pushes me toward the door. "Go, LeeLee. I'm fine. I have a caretaker, and Jameson will be here momentarily to watch me like a damn hawk. All of you, I swear. I'm pregnant, not incompetent."

"Yeah, but you also don't realize what you can and can't do."

She grumbles and mumbles something I can't make out while she rubs and hand over her stomach. "Just go. I'll be alright here. I promise. Look, see? Here comes Jay now." Her chin juts toward the door just as Jameson waltzes through it.

His eyes absolutely twinkle as he looks at Liv, making a beeline for her and kissing her on the forehead while wrapping an arm around her waist and resting his hand protectively on her stomach.

"You ready, Alina?" His mouth pulls into a half smirk as I'm sure he realizes how not ready I am. Several months ago, we had a sit-down and he tried to convince me to get help then.

"Not even a little. But let's do it."

Jameson laughs while Liv shakes her head and Cam throws his arm over my shoulders, pulling me into his side and kissing the top of my head.

"We'll be back in about two hours. Call me if there's any trouble, and I'll come to help out." Cam plans to stay nearby while I'm in my session.

My throat is tight, and I can't get any more words out. This is really it.

Once we're in the car, my knee starts bouncing incessantly and I pick at the dry spots on my lips.

Cam's hand lands on my thigh and I turn to look at him. "It's going to be okay, Ali. Good even. I think you'll find that out quickly."

"It's a lifetime's worth of stuff to dive into. Many of the worst moments of my life. How is that going to be okay?"

"You won't do all that today, for one. Secondly, sometimes it's good to talk about those things. It helps you get them out, get them off your chest, and most importantly, dig deep about why and how they still bother you. I know it seems odd, but I promise it helps."

"It's just the things I try to keep buried that I have to dig up. That's what I'm worried about." And there's a lot that I have deep down that goes beyond the death of my parents and Cam leaving me.

"I can understand that but give it a chance before you judge it too harshly."

The rest of the ride is spent in silence, and once we arrive at our location, I stare at the small office building, working on gaining the courage to open the door.

"I promise to be right here when you're done."

"You're not coming in with me?" I look over at him with wide eyes.

"No." He takes my hands in his and squeezes so I make direct contact with his gaze. "You can do this, Ali. I know you're nervous, but you've been through so much worse. You're stronger than you realize."

At hearing his words, my spine straightens, and my shoulders pull back. I can do this. *I can do this.*

Leaning across the dash, I press my mouth against his. "Thanks for the pep talk. It helped."

With my shoulders still back, I exit the car and take a deep breath before walking across the sidewalk and into the building. Thanks to the directory in the entrance, I find Dr. Stein's office easily.

One more deep breath, and I let myself into the waiting room.

There's nobody at the desk and the entrance is deserted. For a second, I look around to make sure I'm in the right place. Before I can question things too much, a woman who I'd peg to be in her mid-fifties walks into the room with a wide smile on her face.

She's dressed in slacks and a blouse, not what I was expecting. I was anticipating a white doctor's coat. I'm also expecting to lie on the couch while I tell her about my childhood. Maybe it's cliche to think that way, but it's all I know.

"Hello. You must be Alina. I'm Dr. Stein, but please, call me Chloe." She extends her hand toward me, and I take it hesitantly. Her warm smile puts me at ease, as does the first name basis.

"Hi, Chloe."

"Follow me, please."

I do silently and take a look at my surroundings. The walls are a pastel blue with pictures of hot air balloons, open fields, mountains, and other landscapes. It's somewhat serene.

When we enter her office, I wait for instruction.

"Oh, please sit. Make yourself comfortable." Instead of sitting behind her desk, she takes a seat in the oversized armchair to the right of the couch.

Tentatively, I sit on the edge of the couch, putting my purse in my lap and crossing my hands against it.

Chloe gives me a once-over and smiles. "So, Alina, I'd like to tell you a little bit about how this works. This is talk therapy and it's just how it sounds. We'll talk things out. Or, I suppose I should say, you'll talk, and I'll listen. I'll ask guiding questions and give some feedback, but my job is to be ears. Somebody to listen to you and help you work through things, but not tell you any answers. Does that sound alright?"

I can't answer due to the lump in my throat, so I nod instead.

"Start by telling me a little about yourself. Also, I take notes. These aren't judgmental notes; they are for me to be able to refer to later on so I can remember details about you and your life. Is that okay?"

Again, I nod, unable to muster even a simple "yes." How am I supposed to now tell her about myself when I can barely talk?

I open my mouth to start, but then close it again, sure I look like a gaping fish. Clearing my throat, I dive in. "I'm Alina Baker, I'm twenty-six, I live in Juniper Grove and have my whole life. I own a café and bakery with my siblings and run it with my sisters. I have two sisters, one older and one younger, and an older brother. We're all really close.

"I run the bakery part of the café and create all the pastries and treats that we have. I also do some baking on the side for parties and things of that nature."

Quietly, I wring my hands in my lap, waiting for more instruction.

"Anything else? Are you in a relationship? What do you do for fun? I'm just trying to get to know you, Alina. There's nothing off the table."

I nod a few times before continuing. "I'm dating my high school boyfriend. Again. We'd been broken up for about ten years before he came back into my life like a tornado, demanding to see me and talk to me and explain his disappearance and absence for so much time." The last part comes out on a long breath and with a little agitation I didn't realize I was feeling. Interesting.

"You seem to have mixed feelings about that." How can she tell?

"I'm not sure he'd like me to explain why he was gone." My lip finds its way between my teeth.

"Anything you say here is completely confidential and only between you and me. You get to choose what you tell him when you leave here. But if you're not comfortable talking about it yet, I understand that too."

Turning to the right, I look out the window. The sun is shining brightly today. Quite different from the rainy spring we've been having. Though that's spring in New York for you. Rain, rain, and oh yeah, a side of rain. Cam told me to embrace the experience. So, I'm going to.

"The big reason I'm here, which I'm sure we'll have many sessions to talk about, is that my parents were...well...brutally murdered when I was sixteen." I take a quick glance at her and expect to see a look of shock, but her face is completely neutral. "I was dating Cameron at the time, and we were in love. Not the puppy dog love, but real, true, eternal love. I felt it with every fiber of my being. He held me together when my parents died. Literally. With him by my side and helping me, in addition to my siblings, I was able to live a mostly normal life." A smile spans my face as I remember life then.

My parents were gone, but my siblings were all back home and Cam and I were better than ever. I had friends, did things, watched Cam play football. Aside from the lack of parents, it was a real teenage life. Or as real as it could be under the circumstances. We didn't live in sadness then. We made the most of our time, of our life together.

The smile drops from my face as I remember what happened next. "Toward the end of senior year, Cam started to be a little distant. I assumed he was concerned about college, which was looming. I was planning to stay close to home and he wasn't. But we figured we could make it work. Then one morning, he was literally just...gone. No calls, no texts, not even a note. His parents avoided me. He had all but disappeared from the face of the earth."

"What had happened?"

"It wasn't until he came back a few months ago that I even found out. He'd had a drug problem. He'd been a football player in high school and had a nasty break junior year. They put him on some strong painkillers, I remember. Well, apparently, unknown to me and his parents, he'd developed a problem, an addiction." I have to clear the lump forming in my throat.

"I still blame myself a little. How could I have not known? We were so close. Together all the time. How could I not have seen that something was amiss?" Glancing down at my lap, I shake my head and my curls fall around my face. "I should have known."

"Alina, lots of drug addicts are good at hiding their addiction. And it sounds like Cam was one of them." Her words fall over me like a coat, but don't make me feel any better. I should have known.

"Well, anyway, he came back and just expected to talk. Like nothing had happened, like he hadn't up and left and been gone for a damn decade with absolute radio silence. And he expected me to just be willing to talk to him like it was any old day of the week and he was coming to say hey."

"But you did, it seems. Since you're together now."

A small smile curls up the corners of my lips. "I did. It took a little while, but he was persistent."

"How did that make you feel?"

"Wanted. Desired. He didn't give up. Every single day, for weeks, he came by at the same time, and every day, my sister, Olivia, turned him away. But he'd order a coffee and a muffin and sit at exactly the same table and eat in silence. Every single day without missing a beat." This isn't what I expected to talk about today, but it feels good, it feels right.

"The only thing now is that I wonder how he can handle his addiction long term. He's been clean for ten years, but what if life gets hard? I mean, it will. His mom just passed away, and I'm not truly sure how he's handling that. I'm not even sure how I am 'cause it hits close to home. I've kind of just been avoiding thinking about it and my feelings about it. Boxing it all into a neat little package." I shift on the couch, readjusting and frustratedly grabbing a throw pillow to fold over in my lap.

"He bailed once when things were hard for him. How do I know that if life gets hard, he won't bail again? Even if he stays sober? How do I know he'll *stay*?" It's a question that's been sitting deep down in my chest that I haven't wanted to give a voice to.

"You have to trust that he will. Relationships require a lot of blind trust. And it can be hard to give when that person has broken your trust in the past. But think of it this way." She crosses her legs and adjusts herself in her seat. "At any given point in time, in any relationship, both people always have the option to leave. Yes, there's marriage and vows and often children. But nothing truly keeps two people together except their *want* to stay together."

Chewing the inside of my lip, I focus on a spot on the carpet and nod as I try to digest what she's telling me. It makes sense. But then my eyes raise to meet hers. "How do I learn to trust that he won't leave me again?"

"I think that's something we have to work on together in future sessions. Normally, I use this first session as a way to get to know you and your history, but you seemed to need to discuss this. Family of origin is something we'll do in our first few weeks, as it helps me assess some background information and where some of your worries may stem from."

"Sorry, I didn't mean to get us off course." My first session, and I'm already fucking things up.

"Not to worry. I'm here for *you*. Whatever you need to talk about is what we'll focus on. We may have a plan in place, and something happens over the course of the week that you need to get off your chest, so we'll focus on that. It's very flexible."

With tight lips, I nod, still feeling as though I've now fucked up.

We spend the last few minutes of the hour talking about my history of mental health, including my siblings and parents. I realize I know very little about the mental health of the people in my life, and that's something I feel like I should change.

When I leave, I shake Chloe's hand and give her a heartfelt thank you, because everything I got out about Cam today has lifted a weight from my chest.

I walk out feeling lighter, freer, and fresh in a way I haven't in ages. Cam's parked in exactly the same spot, and I wonder if he found it again or if he just stayed in the car for the whole hour.

As I get back in my seat, he sets his phone down. "Hey, how was it?"

Instead of answering, I lean across the center console and take his face between my hands, pulling his mouth to mine. "It was actually really good."

He pulls away with a smile and starts the car back up as we both buckle our seatbelts. "Anything you want to talk about?"

"I do, but just not now."

"That's okay. Whenever you're ready, I'm here." He runs a hand through his golden tresses and looks over at me a few times before putting the car in reverse.

We drive back to Juniper Grove making small talk, but Cam holds my hand the whole time. And instead of feeling nervous about next week, I'm looking forward to my next session.

Chapter 24

Cameron

I truly thought that losing Mom would get easier as each day comes and goes. But I was very wrong. If anything, it's harder.

There are days that I want to go over to see her, to tell her something interesting or exciting or just talk to her, and I have to remind myself that she's not there anymore.

As much as sinking into Alina, both sexually and mentally, helps, my mind still wanders because my heart still aches.

I caught myself wondering how hard it would be to score, if the guy who used to deal to me was still in Juniper Grove, and if he was, how would I find him. At least not without raising suspicion.

That thought process shook me, and I called Spencer right away. While I've told Alina that I've been tempted, that it's hard with Mom gone, I haven't gone as deep with her. I know I need to, I know I should, but I'm worried she doesn't quite understand the depth of it yet. And I'm honestly scared to tell her.

She's going to find out soon enough, as she agreed to come to a meeting with me. Even if she doesn't hear anything directly from me, as

I'm not sure I'm going to speak at the meeting, the things others share will be incredibly insightful for her.

It's become much easier for her to sense when I'm off. Or, maybe not so much for her to notice, but she does something about it. A little shoulder bump, sliding her hand into mine, resting her head on my shoulder. All reminders that she's here and that I can talk to her.

Being with her at the café and watching her bake makes things easier. It's a welcome distraction. She's just utterly captivating in her movements. They're so fluid and rhythmic, like she's following music that only she can hear.

And the winks she shoots me across the room are also amazing. To know that even in her element, fully engaged in whatever delicious treat she's crafting, she's still thinking about me. It makes all the worries drift away, even if only for a moment.

When she puts her third batch of muffins in the oven, it's my cue to leave. We've worked out a solid routine, and by this point, the café is roughly twenty minutes from opening for the day. Liv will have all the coffee brewed and ready for customers, and Alina will pull these new muffins fresh from the oven to start the morning.

I push off the counter I've been leaning against and walk over to Alina, where she's wiping her hands on a towel. Looping one arm around her waist, I tug her against me and kiss her temple.

She leans into me, her body melding against mine. "I hate when it's time for you to leave."

A smile pulls up the corners of my lips. "I love you, Ali."

Her fingers tighten into the front of my shirt, and she nuzzles her nose against my neck. "I love you too. You'll be back later?" She asks this every so often, and I know it's still in response to my leaving years ago. It's going to take work for her to get over, and I'm willing to put in every second.

"Of course. Starting and ending my days with you are the best parts."

"Mmm. Mine too." She pushes up onto her toes and presses her lips against my jaw before she pulls from my embrace.

Before she can get too far, I grip the back of her neck and pull her into me, crashing my mouth against hers. If there's one thing I've learned in all of these years, and especially lately with Mom's passing, it's that there's never enough time.

And I want Alina to know every second of the day that I love her.

With a final peck to her forehead, I back out of the door and into the café. The nutty aroma of coffee fills my senses. I've continued to make sure that I not only remain a paying customer, but that I take on that role on the proper side of the counter.

"What can I get for you today?" Liv looks at me with a smile, a hand on her large belly. She's due any day now, from what Alina said.

My eyebrows scrunch together. She knows my coffee order. "Um, a large black coffee?"

"Sorry, we don't have that anymore."

Confusion swirls within me. There are about ten different carafes behind her, all filled with varying flavors of coffee. And not having regular coffee? Really? "You don't have regular coffee today?"

"Not anymore, no."

"Uh, alright." I drag the word out, not really sure what's going on or what sort of game Liv's playing with me. "Can I ask why?"

"We decided that it was a boring drink order and wanted to fancy it up a little." With a smile, she points to one of the signs behind her.

My heart immediately beats faster as I recall our conversation weeks ago when Alina made fun of my coffee order. Trailing my gaze down the menu, I find it. Caffé Camerlina, in blue chalk. Written next to it in small lettering it says, "Regular coffee."

"I guess I'll take a Caffè Camerlina then," I say with a laugh.

"Excellent choice. New on the menu. Our baker named it for somebody very special." Liv winks at me as she turns around to pour my coffee.

I turn my gaze to the door, hoping Alina's standing right behind it and knows I'm here thinking of how incredible she is.

While I'd love nothing more than to spend the day with her, whether in the kitchen or at her house, a day of phone calls awaits me. At the very least, I have my Caffè Camerlina to keep me company and remind me of my girl.

Chapter 25
Alina

The café's been closed for over an hour and Cam hasn't shown up yet. No call, no text. I'm trying to keep my hands busy by prepping for tomorrow, but it's not helping.

After trying to talk myself out of it for fifteen minutes, I grab my phone and call Liv. She answers on the fourth ring and sounds sleepy as she says, "Hello."

"Sibby. Did Cam say anything about being late today?"

"No. Why?"

"He's not here yet. He usually gets here right when we close up."

"Maybe he got stuck in traffic?"

"In Juniper Grove?" I mean, there's literally one stoplight in the whole town.

"Have you called him?"

"No."

"Why the hell not?"

"It seems too needy."

A heavy sigh fills my ear. "Listen, I love you, but I'm exhausted and trying to nap my big pregnant ass off. Call him." The line clicks dead before I get to say anything else.

"Rude." I look at the phone as though she can hear me through the disconnected line.

Instead of calling, I shoot off a quick text. *Hey. You coming by tonight?*

In the few minutes it takes for him to respond, I nearly chew my lip off. *Yeah. Sorry. Got distracted. Doing some thinking. I'll be there soon.*

It immediately clicks where he is. *No. Stay there. I'll come to you.* My heart pounds in a panic as I worry that he's done something that can't be undone. As I race around the room to get everything situated and grab my things, my breath becomes hard to come by.

Before leaving, I rest a hand against the counter and double over, trying to get deep breaths. There's no reason to think he's done anything reckless, but at the same time, I can't get my mind away from that ledge.

I quickly lock up the café and hop into my car, heading to the one destination I know he'll be.

It's only a few minutes later when I pull into the park. Though it's getting dark out, the days are longer, and the setting sun casts an orange glow around me.

As I near the water's edge, I see him sitting there, curled in on himself and staring out over the lake.

He looks up as I drop to the ground next to him. His blue-green eyes twinkle as he takes me in. "You knew where to find me."

"It's our spot. Right?"

"I wasn't sure you remembered."

"Of course I do. It was always your favorite place to think. Or make out." I bump my shoulder into his, but his lips barely tip up. "What's wrong?"

"It was just a rough day. Lots of bad phone calls, and then I checked on Dad, and he was just beside himself. I mean, I get it, I miss her too. But it was hard to see."

"Did you..." I'm not sure how to ask this, but I know that I need to. "Did you use at all?"

"No. I thought about it. The urge is definitely there. But I didn't seek anything out."

"Have you...have you ever done that...here?"

"No. It's too special of a place for us. But I would be lying if I said I never took you here while high."

I pull my knees into my chest and rest my cheek on top of them. "I wish I had known you were struggling then, Cam."

"I couldn't put that on you. There was enough you were struggling with. Besides, with how it went with your parents..." His chin drops, and as he shakes his head, a few strands of hair fall into his face.

"Trust me, I understand where you're coming from. But I loved you. Unconditionally. I don't know. We're in a good place, but things might have been so different." I can't help but wonder where we'd be now had he stuck around. Would we be married? Would we have kids? Would I even own the bakery?

I can't even imagine not being an owner of Three Sticks, but part of why I dove into the venture and gave it so much of my undivided attention was because I *needed* somewhere to focus my energy and broken heart.

He reaches out and wraps his fingers around my forearm. "There are so many things I'd change, Ali. But I can't. All I can do now is try to move forward with you."

We stare into each other's eyes for a moment, and all the years meld together. All the times we've spent here, in this very spot, rush through my mind, and all I want is to be snuggled up with him.

"Are you ready to go home?" I've stopped referring to it as my house. I rarely did anyway, since it is, in fact, my home, but it's basically become Cam's as well.

His gaze turns back toward the lake. "Maybe just a few more minutes."

This has always been his place to think. I don't remember when he found it, but I know he took me here once when we first started dating and told me he often came here when he had a big decision or something was bothering him. It became a place we would come to together to share our feelings or just reflect on life. He took me here every day after my parents were murdered.

"Whatever you need."

Without another word, he hooks his arm over my shoulder and pulls me into his side, kissing the top of my head. It's peaceful here, just the two of us. All the noise disappears as I focus on the lowering sun, casting beautiful hues of pink and orange across the water.

Chapter 26
Cameron

Alina's been almost a different person since she started therapy, and I couldn't be happier. While it's only been three weeks, she hasn't had a single other nightmare, which I've been worried about since Mom passed. I was afraid it'd hit too close to home, and they'd return with a vengeance, but so far, so good.

I don't know what she talks about in therapy, she hasn't wanted to tell me yet, and that's okay because I won't push. But tonight is the meeting that I wanted her to join me for, and I'm just hoping she doesn't see me differently after this.

Nothing too intense should happen tonight, just a few people sharing. I haven't decided yet if I'll be one of them. There are things I'm thinking and feeling and would like Alina to know, but I don't want her to think that I can't tell her when it's just the two of us. It's more that I feel the need for the support of my community.

I don't want her thinking that her support isn't enough, because it is, but it's still new and a delicate balance. The community has been there for me through some rough times and possible setbacks. With Alina back in my life again, Spencer said that she's basically a new friend since I'm not who I was when we first dated, and not just because I'm an adult now.

Today it's my turn to be restless. Alina's still a little antsy when it comes to therapy, but she comes out seemingly lighter.

"Cam. Calm down, it's going to be fine." I stop my pacing around Alina's bedroom as her words hit my ears.

She was kind enough to leave work early today so that we could get ready for the meeting, with enough time to get there and be a little early, seeing as it's two hours away. It's been a bit since I've seen the group, and I want to be sure that I have a little time to socialize and introduce Alina before we just jump in.

Running a hand through my hair, I shove the other in my jeans pocket. "Sorry. I'm just a little nervous."

"You're going to wear a hole through my floor."

"Sorry."

"You said. Okay. I'm ready." She steps out of her closet and stands in front of me looking amazing in just simple jeans and a pink t-shirt.

"Beautiful. I'm such a lucky bastard."

Her cheeks pinken, and she looks down at her shoes, tucking a curl behind her ear. She's never taken compliments well.

Extending my elbow, I raise one eyebrow. "Shall we?"

She giggles as she hooks her hand over my forearm, and I lead her out of the house, opening the car door for her. Mom instilled a certain type of manners, and Alina deserves for me to learn new ones.

Though I know how far away I live, for some reason, it hadn't clicked that we'd be driving over two hours in each direction. I should have calculated for this and planned something to talk about. Instead, my mind is running wild with possibilities.

Including the fact that if Alina decides she doesn't want to see me anymore, it's a two-hour drive back while stuck in the car together.

She pulls my hand from where I'm playing with my lip and links our fingers together. "Hey. It's going to be okay, Cam. Just like you kept telling me about therapy. I'd be lying if I said I wasn't a little nervous to see what this is all about, but I'm invested because it's for you."

A lightness settles in my chest and starts to drive away some of the dark thoughts that had begun to overtake, making it easier to breathe.

"I know. It's just, there's a lot on the line here. What if you hear some stories and decide it's too much for you?"

"What if I hear some stories and it makes me respect you even more?"

I glance at her quickly to see a quirked eyebrow. She has a point there.

"There's a lot I still don't understand, Cam. Including why you left without a word and were gone for so long. If I can gain even a little insight, I'd like to have it."

The heaviness settles on me again. "I thought you forgave for me that?"

"Just because I've been able to re-establish a relationship with you doesn't mean that I understand the why behind your leaving. Or being gone. I love you, that never changed, and you coming back threw that in my face and reminded me how much and why nothing in my past has ever worked out, but that doesn't erase all the concerns."

While Alina is a very intelligent person, the way she's wording this doesn't sound like her. "Have you been talking about this in therapy?"

She pulls her hand from mine and looks out the window. "Is it a problem if I have?"

I reach for her hand and grab it back, bringing her knuckles to my lips. "Of course not. I just wish you would have said something. You're having concerns about me, about us, and you didn't share that with me."

"It's about trust, Cameron. I'm still working on rebuilding that with you. You've done a lot to show me that I can trust you again, and I think tonight is going to further that, but I can't help but be hesitant about going in blindly again. I need to be careful and guard myself. I'm not sure I'd be able to handle it if you left without a word again."

Her words drive straight through me like shards of glass, slicing their way through all my vital organs and leaving me aching. Foolishly, I thought we were beyond that point. What hurts is that we're at two very different places than I thought we were.

"I'm not going anywhere, Ali. *Nothing* will have me leaving you again. I swear."

"I want to believe you. I do. It's just hard because I thought we were solid last time. The very foundation I stood on cracked and fell apart beneath me. This time, I'm being a little wary."

A harsh swallow hurts all the way down as I try to form words. "I understand."

On some level, I comprehend everything and get where she's coming from. But on the surface, I thought we were beyond that point. That's my fault for not seeing things more clearly and not being more attuned to her. Or maybe for not having a conversation to begin with.

It's like we fell back into the relationship and started where we left off as though no time had passed. But time *did* pass. Lots of it. And we went through a lot of things in that time frame. While we've had discussions about that time, we haven't dug deep enough yet. I'm just now realizing that, and possibly to my own detriment.

It means I'm more invested in this than Alina is. I've jumped in feet first with nothing holding me back, but she's still got one foot on dry land, ready to jump ship if she feels too nervous.

This new revelation makes tonight feel ten times more important than it did when we left, and it has my pulse skyrocketing.

Once we get there, she'll see. Hopefully, she'll understand.

We arrive with ten minutes to spare, which is perfect. It gives me the opportunity to make introductions. She's nervous. I can tell by the way she clings to my hand and half hides behind me.

Alina's never been the most social girl. She'd rather hole herself away in the kitchen than be around other people. While I like being around others, I'm happy to lock myself away with her and only her.

"Lastly, Alina, meet Spencer, my sponsor." I rest my hand on her lower back as I extend the other one toward the heavily tattooed, dark-haired man to my right.

"Hi." There's a waver in her voice that's been there since we got here. She's putting on an air of comfort, but I know she's anxious. I just appreciate that she's here for me.

"Nice to meet the girl this guy can't stop talking about." Spencer claps me on the shoulder with a large hand and my face heats.

"Oh really? Can't stop talking about me, huh?" She looks up at me with a raised eyebrow, but there's a twinkle in her eye as she squeezes my hand between both of hers.

"Well, the little we chat these days. How you holding up, man?"

"As well as I can. Ali's been a big help." I hug her into my side, needing her closer to me.

Before we can talk much more, the meeting is called to order and we all take a seat. Introductions are made for new members, and a few people share. Mostly, I tune it out as I sit with my knee bouncing endlessly. It's not until Alina puts her hand on my thigh that I calm.

"Anybody else want to share?" Jim, the coordinator, asks.

I stand. "I would."

Alina's eyes widen as she looks up at me, her hands folded neatly in her lap.

"Alright, go ahead, Cameron."

"So, I've been doing well for about a decade. There's been a few hard times here and there, but with your support, I've been okay. But my mom passed away recently." A rumble of expected *sorrys* carry around the circle. I look over at Spencer, who nods at me to keep going. "Things have been hard since then. There's a never-ceasing pain in my chest." My fist comes up to my heart as I take another breath. "My mind is constantly going over all the things that I could have done, should have done. What if I'd been around more? What if I never had the addiction in the first place? Lots of things working over and over in my mind."

I startle and look down to my left as Alina takes my hand. I haven't shared this with her. Why, I don't really know, except part of me still wants to protect her from the painful things in life. I don't want her to experience my pain with me.

"It's making the pull to pills stronger. I'm finding myself craving that numbness in a way I haven't in a long time. I've talked to my sponsor more in the past few weeks than I have in probably the last three years, at least about addiction and not football."

A small chuckle fills the crowd.

"While it's helping, I'm still a little anxious, still wanting the numbness. I have an amazing girl in my life, and she's by my side, but I'm honestly a little nervous to confide too much in her, afraid I'll scare her away if I let her know how frequent the thoughts and urges are." Though she pulls on my arm, I can't bear to look at her. Why I haven't told her this, I really don't know. I should have, I know I should have, but fear has taken hold of my tongue.

Not really knowing what else to say, I take a seat and bring Alina's hand briefly to my mouth before settling it in my lap. I'm still unable to even glance in her direction.

"It's okay to have the thoughts and feelings of needing to use. It's not okay to give in. Lean on your partner. That's the most important thing. We're a great community, but we're not part of your day-to-day like your partner is."

"That's great advice, Trey. I'd like to add, as your sponsor, that I'm always here, but he's right. You need to lean on somebody who's with you daily. And I think you'd be surprised by the support you get." Spencer winks in my general direction, but I can tell he's looking at Alina too.

Nobody else speaks up, but they're right. I have to learn to lean on Alina, to confide in her when things are tough and hope that she can be the one to pull me away from the demons wanting to devour me whole.

Chapter 27
Alina

C am's meeting was quite informative. The biggest issue I had was with what he shared. We've been silent on our drive back home for about forty-five minutes, both processing what happened.

"Why didn't you tell me you've been struggling?" It's time I break the silence with the question playing on repeat in my mind. At a certain point, I'd thought it so many times, I was sure I'd said it and he just ignored me, but then I realized he'd never not respond to me.

"I was scared, Alina."

"Of what?"

"Of you realizing that my wanting to use is real. That it means I'm really an addict and can relapse. The idea is one thing, but actually living through it is another." His tone is urgent, but his voice is low.

"But how can we ever really be in a relationship if you won't confide in me about one of your biggest concerns? I understand being scared; I am too. But hiding things from me, especially about this, that's not going to fly this time, Cameron." I need to be harsh and stern. I can't handle secrecy around this again. Not even the possibility of it.

"You need to either be all in, telling me everything, or we need to not be together. I can't handle the fear that you're going to lie to me about this and leave again." A sting settles behind my eyes, and I lift my chin.

"I know. I do. And I should have talked to you. Doing it in the meeting wasn't the right way. I'm sorry. I just...the community has always been there for me, and I felt like I needed their support for some reason. I didn't, I don't. You're all I need, Alina. I swear."

"I don't want you to not be part of the community. I'll make more of these trips with you if you want me to, even if I just read a book in the car or do some shopping or grab a coffee. But it needs to be *both*. I knew nothing about what you were talking about. I had no idea you were struggling *this* much. Maybe that was stupid of me, maybe I should have been more aware or more astute or just assumed a hardship like losing your mom would bring up those thoughts, but I didn't. I'm just happy to know now."

"Can we move past this? Are you going to be able to trust that I'm coming to you?" He glances in my direction a few times and even in the darkened car, I can see the fear in his eyes, hear it in his voice.

I take a moment to think about what I want to say. "I need to know that you're coming to me, Cam. You need to *talk* to me. And don't feel like you need to hide when you call Spencer. If you want privacy, that's one thing, but I feel like you're trying to shield me from it, and that's not okay. I can't feel like you're hiding things from me." That's what this all boils down to. For me to truly trust him, he needs to be a completely open book.

He's nodding before I even finish. "I can do that. I will do that. I'm sorry I didn't already." Frantically, he grabs my hand and links our fingers. "I want this to work this time, Alina, and I'll do anything I can to make sure that it does. Whatever you need from me, I'll do. If that's being open and honest, I can do that. I *will* do that."

"No more secrets. None."

"Not a one."

By the time we get back home, I'm exhausted. The trip itself wasn't terribly long or far, since two hours in each direction is nothing really. But my anxiety was high and that always tires me out.

It's not until my stomach grumbles that I realize all we had was some terrible coffee and stale donuts. It wasn't their fault; it was ours for waiting until the end. Well, on the donuts, at least, not sure anything could have fixed the coffee. Then again, I'm spoiled with Liv's.

Despite the clear hunger in my stomach, I'm too exhausted to eat. "I'm sure you're hungry, because I am too, but I'm way too tired to cook anything."

"I feel the same way. I'm fine to just go to bed." It's early, around nine, but considering we'll be getting up for the café at five, it doesn't feel too soon for sleep.

"Good, me too."

Once we're changed and in bed, I'm lying facing him, my eyelids heavy but unable to stay shut. His hand is working a circuit up my back and along my hip while my fingers trail along his defined abs.

"Thank you for coming with me today." His voice is a low, sleepy rumble.

My eyes raise to meet his, and I'm immediately lost in them. "Of course, Cam. I wouldn't have missed it. And I think it was good for me to see, to hear some of the other stories and see the community you have. It helps me understand a little bit of what you go through."

His hand grips my hip tightly, and he tilts me toward him. "Well, regardless of the why, I appreciate it."

There's an intensity in the air that practically crackles, and before I can take a breath, his mouth is on mine, moving forcefully. He scooches closer so our chests are pressed against one another's as he pushes my mouth open with his, tongues clashing and colliding.

As he lowers me to my back, his hand glides down my thigh, hooking behind my knee and pulling my calf over his waist. With a slight adjustment, he's between my thighs, resting on top of me with just the right amount of pressure.

My fingertips run down his chest, stopping at his pants, and he drags his rock-hard erection along my clit, which causes me to moan. He nibbles at my lip and glides his tongue across it. "I love the sounds you make."

"Well, keep going, and I'll make more."

A devilish smirk pulls up one corner of his mouth, and he lifts the hem of my t-shirt, immediately sucking one of my nipples into his mouth. My arms wrap around his head and hold him tight against my chest, and I grind my hips, rubbing right on his cock.

My other leg hooks over his hip to meet the first, and I lock my ankles behind his back. I writhe beneath him as he lavishes my nipple with his tongue, crying out in pleasure when he takes the other between his fingers and groans against my chest.

He uses his hands to pry mine from around his head, pulling me up to sit as he tears the shirt from over my head before pushing against my shoulder so I fall back to the bed. His hands immediately lower to yank my panties from my body, and I quickly cross my arms against my chest and cover myself, feeling self-conscious at his scrutiny.

His brows pull together, and he wordlessly moves my hands to my sides, holding them against the mattress by my wrists. "Don't you dare ever hide from me, Alina. You're stunning, and you're mine, and I want to see every inch of your perfection."

To further enforce his point, he bends and smoothes his tongue along my hip bone, around my belly button, up my chest, and loops around my nipple before sliding to my earlobe.

A low growl grumbles through his chest and into my ear as he grinds his hips into mine.

I moan as his hand slips between our bodies and his fingers glide through my wetness, his breath hitching. "So wet." He lowers his body so his face is nestled between my thighs and runs his tongue up my pussy and around my clit, making me gasp. "And so delicious."

Wrapping his lips around my clit, my fingers dive into his hair and yank him closer, needing more as he laves me with his mouth. "Fuck, Cam." The words come out as a whine as I wriggle and buck against his mouth.

Pushing away from me, he backs off the bed and quickly strips off his pants and boxer briefs, standing there staring at me with a hungry look in his eyes as he gives himself a few rough jerks.

He takes my foot in his hand and starts kissing at my ankle, working his way up my leg and hooking it over his shoulder. Without hesitating, he plunges his cock into me, driving so deep I cry out and grip at his biceps.

He lowers to his forearms and brushes a hand over my hair. "God, you feel incredible, Ali."

Slowly, he starts pumping into me. Despite the speed, it feels amazing, and every thrust in, I'm gasping for air. Cam has always filled me in a way that nobody else could even come close to.

"Faster."

One corner of his mouth quirks up, and he picks up momentum, thrusting into me hard and fast. He lets my leg fall to the side and pulls the other one up so I'm spread wide for him.

Dipping his hips, he presses in with a new angle, and my back arches as I whine beneath him. He knows that I'm close and that he's prolonging giving me the pleasure I'm so desperately seeking.

"Cameron, please."

He stops thrusting and holds himself above me, his gaze adoring my face. "I love when you beg me. Do it again."

"Please. I want to come. You're intentionally not letting me."

"Now the question is, do I be nice and let you, or do I be mean and keep edging you?"

I whimper in response and try to press my feet against his ass, but the way he's holding my legs, I can't reach.

So I do something instead to make *him* weak. I reach my hand between our bodies and grab his balls, massaging gently. Slowly, he eases into me as his head tips back with a groan.

"Now that I literally have you by the balls. Be nice and make me come."

Instead of responding like I'd hoped he would, by fucking me relentlessly into the mattress, he smirks and pulls out, releasing my legs so they flop to the bed and opening my hand to remove it from his body.

Though I try to keep my hold, he's too strong and can pry my fingers apart easily. For a moment, I'm not sure what's happening and wonder if he's going to just leave me on the edge for the night. He's done it before. But he grabs my hips and flips me to my stomach, pushing my knees under me so my ass is high in the air.

His hands run up the backs of my thighs, over my ass, down my back and into my hair, pulling back so I push up onto my hands. "One of my favorite ways to see you, Ali."

Without another word, he plunges down into me and curses under his breath as all of mine is stolen from my lungs. It may be one of his favorite ways to see me, but it's one of my favorite ways for him to fuck me. Something about the angle lights up every possible sensitive spot inside me, reaching so incredibly deep.

He wraps his fingers tightly around my hips, digging slightly into the bone as he slowly pulls out before slamming back in. Repeating the process over and over, I'm gripping the sheets and whining with every thrust.

When he starts to move faster and harder, my chest drops, and my mouth stays open as I moan with each movement. His hand reaches around, his finger finding my clit, and I disintegrate beneath him.

My body trembles as I scream his name and clamp down around his length, savoring the sound of his breath catching as he pulsates inside me.

"Fuck, Ali." He leans over my back, and I collapse to the bed with him falling on top of me.

We lie there as a mangled mess of limbs for a few minutes, breathing hard as we collect ourselves.

His lips caress my shoulders as he kisses from one to the other. "You're so fucking sexy."

I roll in his embrace, and he leans half over me, brushing a curl behind my ear. "I love you."

"I'm so fucking in love with you, Ali, that sometimes I think it might kill me. I was sure it would if we didn't end up together again." There's such intensity in his gaze that I know he's telling the truth.

His hand runs down my arm, and he links our fingers, watching the trail as he moves.

The thing is, I understand the feeling he has. Sometimes thinking of him hurts in a way. Not a bad way, but a deep, longing pain, even when we're just apart for work for the day. It's different than the ache that used to be there, because now Cam's back and I know it will be remedied soon.

It's almost as though my heart knows that it will be whole again once we're back together, but each morning it tears a little as we separate. Though that seems completely codependent, which is not something I ever expected of myself, it's like when Cam and I reunited, we sealed back together. We'd been so inseparable when we were kids, it's like we reverted back to that.

Regardless, I love him wholeheartedly. I just hope the trust I need to have in him can follow.

Chapter 28
Cameron

Proposing to Alina after a few months of getting back together is a crazy thought. Or is it?

Regardless, it's one that's been rattling around in my brain for a few days now. Ever since she came to my meeting, and the incredible sex we had that night, I've been thinking about it.

She sees me now, all of me, and she still loves and accepts me. I've been able to talk to her about my day and how it's going. We're still digging through Mom's belongings, but it's easier now that I can tell her I'm having a hard moment. She's even come to notice them herself, pulling me away from whatever I might be doing and wrapping her arms around my shoulders, telling me to breathe.

It's not until she does it that I realize I'm elevated. It's easy to get lost in the chores that lie ahead of us. But she pays close enough attention to realize that I'm not on level ground anymore. There's still some getting used to it, mostly because I've been dealing with these feelings by myself for so long and haven't had anybody be concerned enough to know before I did.

It's just one more way Alina's special and meant to be mine. The distracting thoughts are real, so much so, that even Dad can tell.

"What's on your mind, son?" We're going through some of Mom's things together this time. It's still hard for him, which I can't blame him for, it's hard for me too. But today, he's here and he's trying instead of locking himself away in the garage.

We all cope in different ways.

"I'm thinking of proposing...actually."

When he completely freezes, I glance over to see his eyebrows high on his head. I'm thankful Dad never lost any hair and still has a full head of blond. It gives me hope for the future of my own hair.

There's a moment of hesitation before a smile spans his face. "I think that's a great idea. Honestly. The little I've seen of her in the past few months, which is of my own doing, you two have seemed truly happy together."

"I took her to a meeting the other night and she just seems to understand me in a way nobody else ever could."

"She always has. It was hard for us to keep your secret all those years ago. We understood the reasoning and did it without question because you're our son, but we've always loved Alina like a daughter." Something takes over his features that looks more like a memory than grieving a loss. But he quickly shakes it away.

"I know, and I still feel bad about that. I tried to talk to mom about it before...well, before. But she refused to hear my apologies and thank yous, just saying I'm your son and that's what you do and that she'd do it all again without hesitation."

He claps a hand on my shoulder. "We both would. I'm just glad you've been on the straight and narrow for a while now."

"I think that's part of why I felt like I could finally come back and try again with Alina. I realized she was single, and I feel like I'm finally in a good place. And now that we're back together and strong and she sees me, faults and all, I feel like I'm finally the man she needs me to be. I couldn't have been this for her a decade ago, or even a few years ago." While I was clean and sober a few years ago, I was still a wreck. I didn't have a steady job, I was going to meetings all the time to keep myself straight, and I barely could take care of myself.

But now, I have a good job, albeit one in a different part of the state. I'm pretty sure I can work remotely and maybe have to pop in here and there. If not, finding a new job isn't out of the question. Anything to be with Alina.

"Well, then I think it's time you had this." Dad walks over to his nightstand and pulls a box out, bringing it over and setting it in my hand.

"What is it?"

"Open it and find out."

Hesitantly, I do. And I'm met with a large glittering diamond on a white gold band. "What is this? It's not mom's." Mom would never wear anything so large or gaudy. It wasn't her style. In fact, I'm not sure I ever saw her wear an engagement ring.

"It most certainly is. She wore it until she got pregnant with you. Then she felt it was too big and she was worried she was going to scratch you with it. So we downgraded to just her wedding band. And as you got older, she just felt like it didn't fit her anymore. She wasn't the same girl I proposed to, and I understood that. But she wanted to keep it for you, in case one day you found the love of your life." There's a wistfulness to his voice, and I know he wishes Mom were here to see this. To be part of this.

It's a strange bond I'll have with Alina that I never expected.

"You know she loved Alina, right, son?"

"I do. I'm sure she told you, but when I took her to the café that day, she gave us her blessing. She knew she wouldn't be here to see it." I clear my throat around the sharp shards of remorse and look over at Dad.

His lips are parted, and his eyes are wide. "No. I had no idea that's what you all talked about. She merely said she had a great time and that it was great to see Alina again. That you two seemed happy and right together."

"I'm sorry. I didn't know she wouldn't have told you. I guess I just assumed—"

He cuts me off with the wave of his hand. "She kept a few things close to the vest in those final days. It seems she wanted that to be a private moment between you three and something I either found out about later or didn't know about."

"Does that bother you?"

"No. There were few things in life your mother didn't share with me. If some of these were things she felt she needed to take to her grave, then so be it."

Silence overtakes us for a minute before I say what we're both thinking. "I miss her."

"Me too, son. Me too."

We go back to digging through piles of clothes in the stillness. Mom was usually the one talking. It's kind of peaceful in a way, to allow the silence for her even though she's not here to fill it.

There's going to be a lot of that now, for Dad especially.

Alina and I will have to make it a point to stop over more, to come be here with him and have dinners. She loves cooking for any reason at all. I'm sure if I mentioned it, she'd be all for it.

"Thanks, Dad."

"For what?"

"Just...thanks."

He nods solemnly, and I know I don't have to give specifics as to what I'm truly thankful for. Maybe he understands that it's everything, my whole life that I'm grateful for. And he and Mom are a large part of why I still have a life to *be* thankful for. Why I have this second shot at things with Alina.

Why I can plan what has to be an epic proposal to show her how much I love her.

The only problem now is keeping it a secret from her.

Chapter 29
Alina

The buzzing and ringing of my cell phone shock me out of sleep, and I sit up, hair in my face, looking for the infernal device.

Since I started therapy, I've had a few nightmares after having an in-depth discussion about what happened, but far fewer than before Cam came back, and I've finally been having restful nights of sleep.

When I grab onto it, I see my sister's beautiful face and my heart is racing. This must be what Liv felt like every time I called her to come help me.

"Hello?" I try to keep the grogginess out of my voice but fail. It is three in the morning after all.

"LeeLee?" She sounds scared and, suddenly, I'm wide awake, swiping the hair behind my head and shaking Cam awake.

"Sibby, what's wrong?"

"It's time. The baby's coming, and I'm scared." Her voice sounds so small. So much smaller than it has all the time she's been pregnant.

"I know, Sibby. But you have Jay. Where is he?"

"I'm here, Alina!" I can tell he just overheard my question as he shouts, then he's much more direct into the phone. "We're on our way to the hospital. You're welcome to meet us there. She's a little freaked out, but I got her."

"I know you do. We'll be there soon." I'm already throwing off the covers and climbing out of bed, looking for a pair of pants to throw on over my panties.

"Can you call Mazie and Eli? I told her to pick one person."

"Of course, already on it." I'm rifling through my drawers to find a shirt to pull on over my sleep tank. Cam's barely sitting up, hunched over his lap as he groans and rubs at his eyes.

The line goes dead, and I immediately flip to Mazie. "Sorry to call so early, but it's go time. Liv's on the way to the hospital. And she's scared."

"Got it. On the way. You want to call Eli, or you want me to?"

"You can. We'll phone tree it."

"See you there." She hangs up before I get a chance to thank her, and I head over to Cam, squatting on his side of the bed.

"Come on, babe. Time to wake up." I run a hand down his back.

"Tired."

"I know, but it's baby time. All hands on deck."

His eyes widen as he understands the gravity of the situation. "Am I even welcome?"

"You know they accept you now. Come on. I want you there, and I think Liv would too."

He stretches with another groan and throws off the blanket, swinging his legs over the side of the bed. It takes him another minute before he's actually on his feet and pulling on clothes.

I giggle and help him. His feet shuffle as he walks over to the dresser where I've given him a drawer for his clothes. I pull out a shirt, and he takes it, sleepily pulling it over his head.

"Come on, babe. Time to wakey wakey." I shake his shoulder and try to rouse him some more. He's always so quick to respond if I have a nightmare, so this doesn't seem like him.

"Sorry. I'm tired. I wasn't sleeping great." Not sleeping well? Is there something going on that's causing *him* fitful sleep?

"I didn't know that, I'm sorry. But come on, it's time to go see Liv and her baby."

"You know it's probably going to be hours right?" One eyebrow cocks up his forehead as he tugs his shirt down.

"And *you* know that the Baker clan will be waiting in the waiting room for as long as it takes."

He sighs heavily and runs a hand through his blond locks. "I do."

When he finally has his pants on, we're ready to leave. He grabs the keys from the bowl by the front door, and I laugh. "Are you awake enough to drive?"

"I am. I think."

I take the keys from his hand and kiss him on the cheek. "Why don't you let me drive this time?"

"Okay." I know if he's giving in, he has to be really tired. Cam always prefers to drive.

We make it to the birthing hospital in Pineville City in just over twenty minutes. I see Liv and Jameson's BMW already parked and Mazie's Honda is a few spots over from theirs. Of course she managed to beat us here. She probably sleeps in her clothes for the next day.

Once we get into the main part of the hospital, we find our way to the birthing wing. The waiting room is empty save for Mazie, who's already pacing.

"They won't let me see her."

"Why?" I envelop Mazie in a hug while Cam stands sleepily behind me, his hand on my hip.

"They're still checking her in."

"Oh, well, they have to do what they have to do first, Maze. Let them get her checked in and situated, and then I'm sure we can go back."

"Did she tell you she doesn't want me in there for the birth?" She did, and I know it's been a topic of contention between them since Liv shared this news.

"She doesn't want me back there either." I hope that this will bring her some peace. It doesn't.

"I've basically been her mother for over ten years. I'm her oldest sister. Hell, we should all be able to be there if we want."

My eyes widen as I take in Mazie's basically panicked self. "Maze. Calm down. Liv is a big girl, having a baby with her husband. She's in very good hands, and I don't blame her for not wanting all of us back there with her. I don't know that I would either."

Now she turns on me with wide eyes. Cam squeezes my hip and backs away, knowing that this is sibling time. "You wouldn't want us there either?" She sounds hurt.

"No, Mazie. This is a big situation and a very private time between a husband and wife. I want Liv to have that alone time. Just like I would want that alone time with my spouse when the baby was born. I love you all tremendously, but I don't want you *in* the birthing room with me. Be here, waiting for when he or she is born and being the first to meet the new baby. But no, I understand Liv for wanting that moment to be between her and Jameson." I try to use my calmest but firmest tone with Mazie. She may be the oldest, but she needs things broken down for her now and again.

"I guess you're right." Her shoulders slump in defeat. "I'm just worried about her."

"You know that nobody is going to take better care of her than Jameson. He's going to make sure she has everything she needs, including a private recovery room."

"I know. I just feel like we should be there.'"

I put my hands on her shoulders and make sure she sees me. "We are, Mazie. We're right here, where we belong. We're here if anything should go wrong. We're here for the second the baby is born. We're here."

She wraps her fingers around my wrists and nods. Mazie always gets a little over the top when something is going on. She likes to be in control and doesn't do well in situations where she has to give it up. It's probably why she isn't in a relationship. She doesn't get to be in full control since it's supposed to be a partnership.

"Uh oh, what does Mazie not have control of?" Eli's voice sounds behind us, and we both turn to face him. Cam watches on with a smirk on his face, knowing the family dynamic better than most.

"They won't let me back yet, and she doesn't want any of us back there while she has the baby."

"Good. I don't want to see that."

Mazie smacks his chest while I giggle, and Cam stifles a laugh.

"What? She's my baby sister. I don't want to watch that for anybody except my own partner if that ever happens." He looks off to the side so quickly I'm sure he thinks nobody would notice, but Mazie and I both do, locking gazes for a brief moment before looking back at Eli.

He's the oldest of us, and it can't be easy for him to watch us finding our happily ever afters while he's had to give up so much of his life for us and he doesn't have what he wants. Does Eli want a wife and family? I don't know, as I've never really asked him.

"Fine. We'll wait out here." She finally acquiesces and you can hear the defeat in her tone.

"I'm sure we can go in to see her once she's all set up. We just have to be patient, let them do what they need to do." For some reason, when Eli says the same thing I did, Mazie relaxes and nods, then moves to sit. It makes me bristle a little. Eli is the one who can communicate with all of us equally. Somehow, he's able to understand all of our individual idiosyncrasies enough to reach us. But it's frustrating when I'm basically ignored.

I take the seat next to where Cam is slouching, and he immediately links his fingers with mine.

"You hanging in?"

"I'm a bit more awake than when we left. Sorry about that." He squeezes my hand, and I look at him as he smiles.

"That's okay. I don't mind." I rest my head against his shoulder, my eyelids feeling heavy.

Snuggled against Cam, with his warmth and cinnamon scent overwhelming me, my eyes drift shut.

It's not until Mazie is shaking my leg to wake me that I realize I've even fallen asleep, though I have no idea how long it's been.

"Hey. Sorry. We can go see her one at a time. Eli and I have already been back. Cam said to let you sleep."

"Cam's awake?" I sit up to find him smiling at me. I thought for sure he'd be asleep too. "You didn't sleep?"

"I did for a little while, but when I woke up, you'd dozed off so I tried to stay very still."

My hearts warms at his thought process. "Okay. I'm going to go see Liv. How long has it been?"

"It's about seven in the morning. So just a few hours. Doctor says she's moving along nicely, but it will be a while still." Mazie answers for Cam and gives the details he doesn't have.

I stretch and stand, heading over to the nurses' station. They direct me back to Liv's room, where I find Jameson pacing, but Liv lying in bed, a smile on her face.

"Hey, Sibby, Jay."

He grunts and waves a hand in my direction before resuming his pacing, and I walk over to sit next to Liv. "How are you feeling?"

"Oh, I'm great now that I have an epidural. Did you know that contractions hurt like a bitch? I jumped on that so fast."

"Why is Jameson pacing?" I lean forward and whisper the question.

She rolls her eyes and waves a hand in his general direction. "He doesn't have any control, and it's driving him crazy."

"Sounds like Mazie out there. She was losing her mind that we couldn't be back here with you the whole time and she just wasn't feeling the lack of control either."

"This is my wife. I should be able to have more say."

"In what, Jay? What is there to have say over? When she decides to come out? You know it doesn't work that way." Liv turns to face Jameson, her tone full of exasperation.

He crosses the room and takes her hand, kissing the back of it. "You're here, helpless, with a needle in your back for pain, about to push a child out of your body, and I'm just supposed to stand here?"

"Yes. That's the process. And hold my hand and be here to tell me I can do this when I inevitably feel like I can't."

Watching the two of them together always leaves me awestruck. They have the sort of relationship I want. They're there for each other and push each other when needed.

Cam and I are so close to that. He finally trusts me completely, and I'm on my way.

"Are you okay, Sibby?"

"I'm doing great now. Really. I'm comfortable and just waiting. He's making me crazy, though." She whispers the last part, but Jameson's right next to her so he of course hears and rolls his eyes.

"Sorry for worrying about you."

Liv rests her hand on his cheek, and they have a moment of staring at each other intensely.

Without having to exchange any words, Jameson takes a deep breath and rests his head on her arm.

"I'm good. I just wanted to see everybody before things really got started. You guys don't have to stay."

"Of *course* we do."

"Well, it will be a while. Doctor said probably a few more hours, at least. So please make sure you're eating. Go out and get something or go to the cafeteria, though I'm sure it's gross hospital food." Her nose crinkles as she thinks about it, knowing it's what's on the menu for her for the next few days. Though she's mistaken if she thinks I won't be bringing some deliciousness from the café.

I already plan to go back tonight and prepare her and Jay's favorite muffins and scones so they have real food to eat. That is, if the baby comes in time.

"Don't worry about us. Focus on you and bringing that beautiful niece of mine into the world safely."

A yawn stretches Liv's face, and she shakes it away.

"I'm going to go so you can rest. Take the time and sleep a little. Get your energy up. You'll need it from what I hear." I shoot her a wink and squeeze her hand as I stand.

Before I leave, I give Jameson a hug. "Take care of her."

"You know I will."

Once I get back to the waiting room, Mazie and Eli are huddled in the corner talking while Cam flips through a magazine.

"She looks good. Seems to be relaxing right now with the epidural. She said we should go eat, and I'm starving."

"Me too. Want to try the cafeteria, or go somewhere?"

Mazie and Eli take that moment to walk over. "Are you talking food? 'Cause we're hungry too if you are."

"Yeah, we were just trying to figure out where to eat."

"I saw a diner not that far from here. If you two are comfortable with leaving?" Eli hooks a thumb over his shoulder and looks between me and Mazie, knowing we'll be the ones who are least likely to want to leave Liv here.

"She said it'd be a few hours, and Jameson has our numbers in case of an emergency, so we can come right back." At least that's my mentality. Mazie is likely to disagree, but I have to give it a shot.

"Mae?" Eli turns to her, and she chews her lip, her eyes glancing to the doors that separate the waiting room from the delivery floor.

"Okay. I think it'll be fine."

"Alright, diner it is. I'll drive." Eli claps his hands and rubs them together.

We pile into Eli's car, Cam and I in the back, and he drives us over to the diner he spotted. Cam's hand rests on my thigh on the car ride over, but he's unusually quiet.

While he has been a bit quiet as of late, I'm trying to chalk it up to processing his mom's passing and not something else. I, of all people, understand that the pain comes in waves, that the processing takes time and isn't over in a day, or week, or month.

Part of me feels like he knows this is a Baker family event, and he's here because he's my significant other, my rock, but otherwise he has no business being around. Which makes me wonder if I should send him home. But no, this is a happy time, and Zachary came when Liv was hurt. Should he also be here now? He's like family.

When we sit, we get coffee all around, though it's surely not going to compare to what Liv makes at the café.

Cam and I lean into each other as we eye the menu, but I almost always get the same thing at a diner. A breakfast sandwich. There's something about the greasiness that just sets me up right for the day. Plus, I rarely make them. But everything else, like pancakes and waffles, are things I whip up for breakfast any old weekend.

When the waitress takes our orders, I go last. "Bacon, egg, and cheese on a hard roll, please. With a side of French fries." I hear Cam mumbling the same order under his breath and laughing as the waitress takes my menu.

His hand lands on my thigh and he squeezes so I look over at him. There's so much sincerity and love in his eyes, it takes my breath away.

It's then that I realize this is the first time Cam's really been with my siblings in the open since he came back and, suddenly, anxiety has me by the throat.

Is this going to be nice and calm? Or are they going to ask questions that they have no business asking?

But instead, we're able to have polite conversation, mostly focused on Liv and how she's doing, how Jameson is likely handling it. Apparently, he was about the same for each of them.

"I get it. He loves her and he's worried about her. It's a stressful situation to have the love of your life be so vulnerable and know you can't control a single aspect and have to just stand by and hope for the best." Cam steals a fry and pops it in his mouth as he finishes.

I stop mid-bite and turn to look at him. It's clear he's put thought into it. But for us? Are we at the point where he's thinking about marriage and kids?

I'd be lying if I said I haven't thought about it, but there are still things that worry me about Cam. It's not even his addiction. He's done a great job so far since his mom passed, and I know it's been a rough road for him.

But life is hard and for more than just the loss of parents. This is one big bump in the road, but one he saw coming. What if there's something he doesn't know about that throws him? Something between us. We haven't really fought at all since we got back together, but that's unlikely to stay the same.

It's my biggest worry. That again, I'm going to give him everything and all my love, all my trust, all of myself, and things are going to be too hard and he's going to split. Only next time, I might not be just me that's left alone.

"Have you...have you thought about us and kids?" I ask the question under my breath so hopefully only Cam can hear me. I'm not sure if that's the case or if Eli gets that this is a private moment, but he turns to Mazie and starts making conversation.

"Of course I have. You haven't?"

"I have. I just haven't landed anywhere yet."

His brow furrows and hurt laces his eyes. "You haven't? I thought you wanted kids."

"I do. But I worry about the longevity of our relationship, Cam. There's still a lot to talk about and work through that makes me hesitate."

He straightens and puts his fork down, running his tongue along his teeth. "I see."

I put my hand on his arm to calm him because I can tell he's getting upset. That what I said, or maybe didn't say, has hurt him. "It's just some things I need to work through with Chloe."

"How about working through them with me, Alina?" He's frustrated, and understandably so. But this isn't the time or place for us to discuss such things.

"We can talk about this later. But know that I love you, Cameron. Completely."

"It doesn't seem like it." My eyes flutter shut at the hurt in his tone.

Reaching down, I link my fingers with his, but he gives a quick squeeze and then pulls his hand back to his lap.

A quick glance at Mazie and Eli and I can tell she knows something is going on by the way her gaze dashes over to me, but she doesn't stop whatever she's talking about with Eli. Something about the semester.

I feel small. Cam's clearly at least hurt by what I said, if not also mad. Mazie knows something is going on and is biting her tongue, thankfully.

The pressure from both of them is suffocating and making me feel like I need to shrink in on myself.

There's some discussion about who pays the check, Cam offering but being denied by Eli, and we leave mostly peacefully. Cam takes my hand as we walk to the car and tugs me into his side, kissing the top of my head. He says nothing but keeps me close to him and opens the door for me.

I'm not sure if he's moved on from what was said at the diner, or is just playing it cool for now, but I'll be on the edge of my seat until I know for sure.

Chapter 30

Cameron

What Alina said at the diner has really thrown me for a loop. I'm thinking of proposing and she's not sure she wants kids with me?

What kind of bullshit is that?

I thought we were in a different place, that things were better after my meeting, and we were on the right path. Now I'm not so sure.

It's obviously a discussion we need to have.

But not while her brother and sister are watching me like a hawk, and certainly not while we await the birth of her niece.

So instead, I bury it deep down. This isn't the sort of thing that can just be brought up casually. We need to have a real sit-down conversation about it.

But I don't want her worrying. I don't want her thinking anything is off right now on this otherwise very happy day.

So I act as normal as I can, holding her hand, kissing her, letting her rest on my shoulder. All stuff I'd do if things were perfect.

She has to know that I'm hurt. There's no way she can read me so well lately and not have any idea that her words, or lack thereof, hurt me. But I'm not letting it show, not today, not right now.

Any time she hesitates to rest her head against my shoulder, I take my hand and press against her cheek so she's comfortable. I stretch my arm across the back of her chair and pull her into my chest. I do what I have to so she knows or feels like I'm comforting her.

And I am. Because I love her and want to be here for her. Especially on this day. I feel special and like I'm finally included in the fold by being welcome today. Not even Zach's here and he didn't disappear for a decade and put a black mark on his record. Though it's possible he's just working and will be here later.

I've had to field a few phone calls of my own, taking the call to a corner of the waiting room or out in the hall. The waiting room has filled a bit more as the day has progressed.

It's only mid-morning, but it appears that at least two more families are here. Though there are TVs and magazines and lots of things to occupy oneself with, there's a lot of pacing that goes on in the waiting room.

Aside from the phone calls, I've mostly stayed seated. I've gotten used to sitting in places for long periods of time and waiting. I try to keep my splayed legs from being in anybody else's way. Alina primarily stays next to me.

Any time the phone rings and I look at it, she peeks over at me, not sure what to make of it. Every time I just mumble that it's work and stand.

It's been a long several hours, and I've seen the same commercial at least three dozen times, advertising a new local restaurant. The amount of money they must have sunk into the ad is insane.

The situation is so mundane and drawn out. I'm happy to be here for Liv, but this waiting is for the birds. It lets my mind wander too much and to too many things, including how numb I'd feel if I could fall into a bottle of pills right now. Sitting up straight, I shake the thought away. I can't give in to those kinds of temptations.

At a little after one, when I'm starting to feel hungry again after the big breakfast we had, Jameson comes through the door. We all stand and crowd around him.

"She's here. Seven pounds, eight ounces, twenty inches long. She's absolutely perfect. Both she and Liv are doing amazing. She was born almost an hour ago. In a few minutes, they're going to be moving Liv up a floor to the nursery. You'll be able to come see us up there." The siblings crowd him and give him a hug.

Patiently, I wait my turn and clasp a hand on his shoulder. "Congrats, man. Big day."

"Thanks. It's all a blur. But she did amazing. Trust me, these girls are rock stars." His gaze drifts over my shoulder to Alina, who I turn to see is gathering our things and clearing away our coffee cups to make the transition up a floor.

"Yeah. I believe it." I try to keep the sadness out of my tone, the weight that's dragging me down away, so he doesn't have anything less than excitement on his big day.

"I'm going to head back. See you upstairs."

"Yeah. See you there." The words barely exit my mouth. It doesn't matter because he's already back through the doors, on his way to his wife and new daughter.

Am I ever going to have this? Will I get this moment to come out and tell the Bakers about the sweet tiny bundle of joy while Alina holds him or her in her arms?

Sure, if Alina and I were to not work out, I could find it with somebody else. But what's the point? I don't *want* a family with anybody else. Just Alina.

A real conversation needs to be had about what we each see for our future. Because if we're not on the same page, I don't want to make a fool of myself by proposing, only for her to say no.

And if she doesn't want to be with me, well, then that may be the push that sends me over the edge once and for all.

Chapter 31
Alina

I t's been three weeks since Liv had her gorgeous baby girl. While we've all gotten snuggle time in, it's surely far less than we're used to seeing Liv. Though people have begged her to bring the baby by the café, she's insisting on waiting until Jordanna is at least two months old.

Ever since the hospital, Cam's been off. I don't want to think he's hiding something from me, but it's impossible not to and my mind goes to the worst place. Is he using again? Is he hiding it from me?

Nothing about our time together has changed, but he has basically the entire day while I've picked up slack at the café in Liv's absence. Mazie's been in a lot too and we've had our staff up their hours.

Cam says he's working during that time, and I believe him, but there's a tiny voice that's nagging at the back of mind, wondering if he isn't also doing something else with that time.

The problem is, I don't know how to bring it up without causing a disagreement. And with how crazy the café is, it's really something I'd rather avoid.

It's starting to wear on me. That and the added pressure at the café. Liv is such an integral part of the equation, it's hard to do it without her. The last time was during her accident, and then we were all just so thankful she was alive, we barely noticed. Now her absence is very much felt.

Cam was going to meet me as usual tonight, but I'm just too tired and text him that I'll see him when I get home early instead.

It means more work to do in the morning, but a good night of sleep feels worth the extra effort tomorrow will bring.

When I walk in the house, Cam's pacing the floor, phone to his ear. I make sure I'm quiet since I assume it's work, but the second he sees me, his face pales and he immediately tells them he has to go and hangs up without an answer.

With a deep breath, I try to bury the question but am just too tired. "Who was that?"

"Oh, nobody important." Not an answer for somebody who's supposed to be building trust.

"Okay." I drag the word out because I'm not sure that it is okay.

"Listen, we should talk." This is it. He's going to tell me something terrible. That he's using again, leaving, both.

"Yeah, maybe we should."

"I wanted to talk about what happened at the diner a few weeks ago. I haven't brought it up because, well, I know things have been hard at the café, but I just can't bite my tongue anymore."

My brow furrows. "Oh. That's what you want to talk about?"

"Yeah, what else would it be?"

I look down at my feet and switch the weight from one to the other as my hands clasp behind my back. "Nothing."

Cam stands in front of me in a second, using one finger to tip my chin up. "Explain yourself."

"I thought you were going to say something about using again. Or planning to leave." The words burn on my tongue as I say them and guilt floods through me. He's given me zero indication that either of these are likely, but I can't help my mind from going there.

He drops my chin and fire rages in his irises as he takes a step back. His ass hits the table and his hands plant firmly on it. His face is shrouded in pain and anger. "You're never going to trust me again, are you? You're never going to believe that I'm staying?"

That's the moment it all falls apart. All the exhaustion catches up with me, and I break. "How could I? You *left*, Cameron. Just up and gone. For years, *years*, I thought it was my fault, that you left because of me. How would I know better? I was a kid, and the boy I was irrevocably in love with was gone overnight and I didn't hear from him again for a decade. It wasn't until now that I learned the truth."

He stays silent as I have a meltdown, the tears pouring from my eyes like rivers that have broken their banks.

"And how am I to believe you wouldn't leave again? That you wouldn't find things to be too hard and relapse? I know your sobriety is important to you. But if life gets too hard, how do I know you won't fall back to it?"

"That's not fair, Alina. I'm an adult now. I have a sponsor and ways to help me. Hell, you came to a meeting with me to see the support system I have." Hurt laces his words, and I know that he's holding back strong emotions.

"It still took you years to come seek me out again, Cameron."

"I told you I thought you were married."

"That was years ago!"

His hand goes to his forehead, and he rubs it with his fingers. "Regardless of any of that, I'm back, and I'm here for *you*. I have always wanted you, Alina. You're the most important thing to me and our kids would be too."

"I'm worried about when things get difficult. Or if you get hurt again. What happens if we have a big fight, or things start to not work between us?"

"None of that matters, Alina. My sobriety and you are way more important than anything. I'd come to you. Yes, it may have taken me a bit to open up, but I am now. You know the difference in me, you *see* it. I'm not going to hide that from you ever again. You're the only thing that matters to me, Alina. It's always been that way, and I lost sight of it at one point and fell. But I was a fucking kid then. I made a mistake. And I've grown up. I'd hope you wouldn't hold mistakes like that against our kids." The way he says 'our kids,' so full of conviction. Like there's no doubt in his mind that we can make it that far.

I chew my lip and look away. I so desperately want to believe him, but I'm struggling. Can people change?

"I'm worried, Cam. I want to believe you and trust you, but I'm not sure how."

"I'm trying to tell you that you don't have a reason to be worried. That you *can* trust me."

"What's with all the secrecy lately then? If you really want me to trust you, then tell me about what you're hiding because I know it's something."

His head drops back with a groan, and he rubs a hand over his face before locking it behind his neck and looking at me with desperation. "Not that. Anything but that."

"Why? What are you hiding?" My voice rises as he looks guilty as sin.

"Nothing bad, Ali. I promise."

"I'm sorry if your word doesn't count for enough just yet."

"That's not fair. I haven't done anything since we've been together again for you not to trust me. Is this really still all from a decade ago?"

While I don't have a definitive answer, it is something I've been going over with Chloe. The whole situation is something we've talked about at length. He left, I have memories of that, and it's easy to feel the same, especially right now while he's hiding things.

"I don't know. I can't honestly answer that question for you. All I know is that my trust has been wavery at best and now you're hiding things from me and—"

"I plan to propose, Alina." He interrupts with words that stop me in my tracks. His voice is eerily calm as he continues. "I've been trying to plan the perfect proposal for you, so I've been in contact with some people to help make it special and keep it secret. I was on with Jameson when you came in. He was going to talk to Liv about possibly having you have a girls' day to get your nails done first."

My eyes flutter shut and my heart weighs heavily. A shaky hand raises to my mouth. I ruined his proposal. Because I can't trust him.

"I have to go."

"What?" His brow furrows together as he tries to puzzle out why I'm leaving.

"I just...I have to go."

Before he can answer, I'm back through the front door. I hadn't even taken off my shoes before we got into the discussion. Argument. Whatever it was.

But now I need to go get some answers and some guidance from somebody who may be able to help.

Chapter 32

Cameron

I can't believe I told her I wanted to propose, and she just walked out.

There are two choices here. Leave and go back to Dad's for the night or stay and wait for her to return and hopefully not throw me out.

I have a pretty strong feeling about where she went. There are really only three places she'd go, but one is who she's closest to. And I think depending on what's discussed, things will turn out in my favor.

Her struggling to trust me isn't something I necessarily blame her for, but the fact that she just up and left when I told her I wanted to be with her forever, that's another story. I'm trying not to be hurt by it, but the pain is seeping through my armor anyway.

Knowing Alina, she just needs some time to think and talk it out. She does best when she can express her thoughts and feelings. Sometimes she just needs to get them out to truly process them.

At least, I hope that's what's going on here.

Does she expect me to leave?

Now I'm not so sure staying is the right course of action.

Instead of deciding, I end up pacing, mumbling to myself about the situation while trying to keep myself from wanting to jump off the deep end.

I adore Alina to a fault, and I know that her trust in me is something she's been working on with Chloe. She didn't want to tell me; it kind of slipped out one time that they were talking about her ability to trust me.

It's a long road back and I deserve to work for it. I just thought we were further than we are. Where she was ready for a long-term commitment instead of still working on the foundation.

None of her hesitation changes my mind, though. Maybe because I understand where it's coming from. She has a history of people leaving her, of *me* leaving her. A few months back and giving her my all isn't enough to erase a decade of being gone, of the initial hurt I caused.

Not to mention her parents left and never returned. Sure, the situation was very different, but they're gone all the same.

If she lets me, I'll prove to her every damn day how much I love her and that she can not only trust me, but *in* me.

Chapter 33
Alina

P arking in Liv's driveway, I stare up at the house. It's one of the nicest, and biggest, in town. And it's always been Liv's favorite. Rumors have circled for months that Jameson knocked on their door one day and offered them a massive lump sum to move out. That's not at all reality, as the Dublon's were in the café a few days before Jameson made the offer, talking about selling.

One thing that can be said about Jameson is he seems to live to make my sister happy. And I couldn't be happier about that. He had contacted the real estate office and told them all that he wanted to know about new listings before they go live. As luck would have it, Liv's dream house went on the market within weeks of that conversation.

Taking a deep breath, I walk to the door and let myself in. It's something Jameson is still getting used to. We've all offered to knock, ring the bell, call first. But he insists that he just needs a little time and doesn't want to change our routines, our connections. Jameson's a one-in-a-million type of man.

What I walk into can only be considered chaos. Liv's standing in the middle of the living room, bouncing her knees while holding my precious niece. The table is littered with bottles, glasses, coffee mugs, burp cloths. I know Liv is breastfeeding, which must mean little Jordanna was giving Liv a hard time and Jameson tried bottle feeding her.

"Hey, Sibby. You okay?"

Whipping around at my voice, my heart drops at Liv's face. Deep circles rest under her eyes. "Oh, hey, LeeLee. Sorry for the mess."

"Nonsense." Taking a step forward, I reach my arms out to the whining, squirming three-week-old. "Want me to take her from you for a minute?"

"She's a little fussy, it's probably better if I just keep her. Listen, you know I love you, but do you need something?" Exhaustion is clear in her tone as she shifts Jordanna from one arm to the other.

"I wanted to check in, see how things are going. I could use some sisterly advice. About Cam." It all comes out a bit hesitantly, and I almost leave the last part out and wait until I'm into the conversation since Liv probably won't feel it's an emergency enough for me to be here right now.

"Well, I'm working on, like, three hours of sleep so I can't promise anything I have to say will be full of wisdom or even good advice, but shoot."

"Mind if I help tidy up while I talk?" Not only is it something I do when I'm anxious, but it will help my sister in a way she needs right now.

"You don't have to do that. We'll get to it."

"I know, but it will help me from overthinking if I keep my hands busy." It's only a slight fib. The tremble that's been residing in my body since I left has vacated for the moment, but I know the second I start talking about this, it will return.

"I'd really appreciate it then." The softness of her voice holds a touch of defeat. As utterly adorable as my niece is, she's been giving Liv and Jameson a run for their money. While Liv is still on maternity leave from the café, we've all told her that if things don't change, she should take more time.

Poor, sweet, baby Jordanna is colicky and up all the time.

Gathering bottles and glasses in my arms, I formulate my words before I dive in. "Cam wants to propose."

She stops in her tracks, and her eyes widen when she looks at me. It takes one wail from Jordanna before she starts moving again.

"Yeah. But I don't know that I can trust him. I know he's been clean for ten years, but he went through all of it behind my back...he kept it from me and then disappeared. How do I know that he won't fall into it again if we try this and it gets hard? Life is difficult, it's messy, it's stressful. Making a commitment? Making a relationship work? It's not easy and I'm afraid he'll fall back into that to cope. I'm worried he hasn't truly changed, that he just hasn't had troubles that he's had to work through. That he can't change." The last part leaves a sour taste in my mouth.

Looking around, I notice I've cleaned off the whole table, straightened the pillows on the couch, folded the blanket, and have a rag against the tabletop. This happens sometimes when I get too into something; I lose track of what I'm actually doing. My therapist says it's dissociating, blocking my mind from the painful or difficult and just going through the motions.

Dropping the rag, I sit on the couch and look at Liv, whose eyebrows are raised as she paces the room, patting Jordanna's butt while she squirms and grunts.

"I don't know, Leen. Jay changed a lot. The second he found out I was pregnant, he sold the Vette, which he swore he'd never do." Pausing in her movement, she stares at the ceiling for a second. "Man, I miss that car," she says low and under her breath.

Shaking away the thought, she starts walking and patting again, eyes back on me. "Anyway, now he's mister family man, driving an SUV with third row seats and DVD players going the speed limit."

"It's a BMW." My head tilts to the side as I point this out because she says it like he's driving around a beat-up minivan instead of a luxury vehicle.

"Still an SUV. And we both know he didn't *need* to sell the Vette to buy the Beemer. Or the Jag, not that he uses it much."

"Yeah, have I asked you yet how you managed to bag a hot billionaire?" A smile pulls up the corner of my lips as I smile at my sister.

"He was apparently attracted to my snarky attitude."

"Oh, so he's crazy."

Taking the burp cloth from her shoulder, she chucks it at me.

"I'm serious, though, Alina. When I met Jameson, he was a true workaholic, set on never getting married. Now? Well, just look at me." Holding the baby in one arm, she waves the other hand down her body while standing in place and bouncing with her knees.

Following her hand, I take her in. Her normally perfect curls are frizzy, wild, and half piled on her head. While she usually wears jeans, lately she dons yoga pants and whatever t-shirt she can throw on. Today, I'm pretty sure it's Jameson's and covered in mystery spots of baby fluid.

Lastly, my eyes zero in on the mega rock on her finger. Honestly, I don't know how she keeps her hand up with that thing.

Before I have chance to say anything, the door swings open and Jameson walks in, a box of diapers in one hand and a bouquet of flowers in the other.

Noticing me, his lips pull into a tight smile. We get along great these days, but he clearly wasn't expecting me to be here on what I'm sure is little sleep.

"Hey, Alina." He holds the diapers up for Liv to see before setting them near the stairs, then walks over to her, wrapping an arm around her waist and bending to kiss her as she tips her face up to his. They've always been like this, moving toward each other and anticipating one another.

"Hey, baby. She giving you trouble?" He's already scooping their daughter out of Liv's arms and handing her the flowers. His face breaks open in joy, and Liv runs a hand over the top of her head. Jameson looks at her as she blows out a breath, his features soft and full of adoration. "I got her. Go shower. Or take a bath."

"Alina's here."

Patting my knees, I stand to leave. "I can go. Really, I got what I came for."

"You're welcome to stay. If I can get her to sleep, I was planning to make a fresh pot of that hazelnut coffee Liv likes so much." Liv perks right up at the words, and Jameson smiles at her.

"No, really. I'm good." Everything I needed I've gotten. It wasn't hard for me to accept Jameson like it was for Eli and especially Mazie. I know Liv the best and I could see, from day one, how smitten she was and how happy he made her. Over a year later, and he still lights up her life, makes her days better. Sometimes it seems like he lives for her and her happiness.

But Liv is right. Jameson prioritized his job and single life above all else when they met. It took them getting together for things to start to shift, and almost losing her forever for him to completely change his priorities. But he has changed. While he is working again, he's made it exceptionally clear that his home base is here, all the time. Any future travel would be minimal to nonexistent with Liv and Jordanna always being welcome to join him.

The change I see most is that Jameson was clear on not expecting to marry, until he met Liv, but was still unsure about kids. The love that man has for his daughter is astounding, and Liv says he's already asking for more. Five of them, to be exact.

Cam has been clean and sober for over a decade. And while he's confided in me the times things were hard, the times he thought about taking pills, he's also being more open and honest than I think he ever was when we were first together.

When his mom passed, it was the first real test for us. And he handled that with grace. Yes, it was hard, but he made it known if he was struggling. I can see the change in him now and know when he needs a little extra support.

If Jameson can change completely, go from something he doesn't want, to embracing those things, then certainly Cam can stay sober.

Chloe has said that my lack of trust in him stems from when he was a kid and that I haven't seen him as an adult. Or least haven't given him the benefit of the doubt as an adult.

I think it's time that finally changed.

Chapter 34

Cameron

I'm about to head out when the door flies open and Alina comes barging through, barreling into me and wrapping her arms tightly around me.

It knocks me back a step, and then I loop my arms around her, lifting her off the ground. She's back and clearly not mad. Which I hope is a good sign.

Setting her down on flat feet, I take a minute to take in her beaming face.

"Ask me again."

One corner of my mouth ticks up. "I haven't actually asked you yet."

Her bottom lip pops out in a pout, and I lean down to bite it.

"Tell me where you went, what happened." I loop my arm around her waist and pull her over to the couch, sitting on the end and sliding her into my lap.

"I went to Liv's." That's what I assumed. Glad to know I was right.

"And?"

"She's a hot mess, but they're getting through it."

"Alina." There's a warning to my tone because she knows she's avoiding the real question.

Her chest rises with a heavy sigh. "I just wanted to talk it out. I know I love you, Cam. But the trust is hard. I've been working on it with Chloe, and she made me realize I'm keeping you locked in that childhood version of yourself who left, not the adult version who came back and has made progress and *shown* me progress. So, I just went to Liv to see if she thinks people can really change." She refuses to look at me, instead playing with an imaginary string on her pants.

"And?" I close my hand over hers to stop her fidgeting.

Her eyes finally meet mine. "I realized that you already have, and I haven't been able or possibly willing to see it, and that's my fault. I've been looking at you as the same eighteen-year-old who left me and never came back. But that's not you anymore. And even though I didn't know about the addiction, that's not you anymore either. You show me every day that it's not who you are, and I need to accept that and actually see it."

Relief floods my chest with her words and my eyes flutter shut. "Sounds like it was a good conversation then."

She gives a small nod. "I was worried that people can't change, but she showed me how Jameson has, including Jordanna. He didn't anticipate getting married or having kids and now he has both and loves his life. The way he looks at her, even covered in spit up, clearly exhausted while holding a screaming newborn, was just full of love and adoration. He didn't seem frustrated or overwhelmed. He seemed genuinely happy. And I thought if he can change, maybe you can too." She trails a finger along my collarbone.

"While I wish it didn't take all of that for you to realize I'm not the same kid I was ten years ago, I'm glad you're finally there." I take a minute to let that sink in before leaning down to brush my lips against Alina's.

She responds immediately, wrapping her arms around my neck and pulling herself straight in my lap. She throws one leg over my lap so she's straddling me, and I lose a hand in her mess of chocolate curls.

My lips press against hers, parting them so my tongue can slip in. They dance together in what feels like choreographed moves, so beautiful and perfect together.

I drag my mouth down to trail along her neck and the curve to her shoulder, moving the collar of her shirt from my path. Every inch of her skin is silky smooth.

Placing my hands under the hem of her shirt, I lift the garment off in one swift movement, tossing it on the floor before immediately unhooking her bra and dropping it to the ground. My hands cup her perfect breasts as I stare into the caramel eyes I love.

I rub my thumbs over her nipples and her head tips back, making her curls cascade down her back like a waterfall of chocolate. Leaning forward, I pull one of her nipples into my mouth, and her hands dive into my hair as she hugs my head against her chest.

My tongue laves at the hardened peak, and she grinds her hips against mine. She's seeking friction, something, anything to give her a little more. So, I reach into my pants and adjust myself, then her, so she's resting right on my cock.

Sinking herself even lower on my lap, she moves herself forward and back, grinding hard against me. I groan against her breast, and she whines as I sink my teeth into her flesh.

"Cam." I love hearing her say my name so full of need and desperation. It does something to me, unlocks a primal instinct that goes wild, needing to have her this very second.

With strong hands, I push her from my lap so she's standing on her feet again. I slink low in my seat. "Take your pants off. Slow and sexy."

A sly smirk spreads across her face and her cheeks pinken. But she does what I say, sliding her hands up her chest, over her breasts, into her hair, and back down her front, where she slowly unbuttons her jeans, shimmying them off her hips and turning around so I get a view of her perfect ass.

A loud smack fills the air as my hand whips out and claps against the firm roundness in front of me.

She starts forward with a small yelp before flipping her hair back and standing straight, wearing nothing but a thong.

Turning to face me, she leans forward, putting her hands on my thighs and stepping between my legs as she runs her hands up until she reaches my dick. She squeezes her hand around my length and my head tips back against the seat cushion with a groan.

Her fingers work quickly at the button and zipper of my jeans, which I lift my hips to lower and kick off.

She's back on top of me in seconds, raising herself so her breasts are in my face and I can pull her nipple into my mouth again. This time, my fingers dip into her thong and run along her soaking pussy.

"Fuck, good girl giving me a little striptease and being ready to take me." I speak right against her mouth and pull her lower lip between my teeth.

With one hand on her hip and the other on my cock, I line myself and lower her onto me. While I try to make it quick, she presses against me to give some resistance and takes it agonizingly slow. But every inch of her feels incredible as she lowers more and more.

Once she's seated, I let go and lean back, crossing my arms behind my head and swiping my tongue along my bottom lip.

Her fingers glide under the hem of my shirt, which I quickly pull from behind my head and toss over the back of the couch. She plants her hands on my shoulders and starts to move herself forward and back on my lap. Within minutes, she adds a slight lift to the movement; forward, up, down, back. Repeat.

Whines ease from her lips with every bump down, and while it feels amazing, and she's making incredible sounds, I need more.

Taking her hips in my hands, I start moving her harder and faster. Her nails dig into my skin, and she moans loudly as I slam her down onto my length.

But it's still not enough. Holding her hips up, I pound into her.

"Cam."

A bit hastily, I pull her off, flipping around so she's bent over the couch and I'm behind her. "Oh, fuck."

Her top half collapses to the couch with a moan as I ease myself inside and hold her hips in my hands. I look down so I can watch as my cock slides in and out of her tight little pussy. It's one of the greatest things I've ever seen.

But slow is not how I want to go right now. So I thrust hard and fast, the sound of skin on skin increasing with every one.

The noises she's making are incredible and fill my ears in the most wonderful way as she grips at the cushions.

"Fuck. I'm going to come."

"Yes, baby. Come on my cock." Just the thought has a tingle settling in my spine and my balls tightening.

When she clamps down on me, I release right behind her, spilling deep inside her with a groan.

I collapse over her back and we both fall to the floor. She giggles as she rolls onto my chest and kisses her way up to my jaw. "I love you, Cam."

"I love you too, Ali. But I'm not going to propose right now."

She pouts and my fingers dive into her ribs and tickle her as she writhes and giggles.

One of the best parts of knowing somebody most of your life is that you learn small details, like their ticklish spots. But also that you see how they grow and change. Alina may be all woman, whereas she was just a young, broken girl when I left, but right now she looks youthful again. I love that I can see the comparison, that I knew the young Alina and now get to know the older Alina.

As her giggles fade, I wrap my arms around her and squeeze tightly, kissing the top of her head. "Let me plan you something special. You deserve it, and I want to do it right."

"I don't need anything more than just you, Cam. Right here, right now, just the two of us is plenty."

"It's not. It never could be. I have a lot to atone for still, Alina, and I plan to do that every day for the rest of my life. But let me start with a proposal to end all proposals." Not that what I have in mind is quite that extravagant. In fact, I'm not really sure *what* I'm going to do.

All I know is that it has to be something amazing, just like Alina.

Chapter 35
Alina

It's been three weeks and Cam still hasn't proposed. I'm on high alert every single day and have gotten my nails done three times. That's more than I ever get them done. I'm more of the au natural type, but Liv said getting a manicure is one thing she had been able to plan for.

This is my last time, though.

If Cam doesn't propose soon, I'm going to assume he changed his mind.

Every day I'm on eggshells, waiting. Any time he touches me I practically jump out of my skin.

He's starting to take advantage of it. This morning we were walking from the car to the café, and he knelt down, grabbing my hand as he lowered. My breath stuck in my lungs and then all he did was ask me to wait while he tied his shoe.

The other day, he said he had to ask me a serious question, his face completely stoic. My heart raced as I thought it was the moment. Then he asked me which tie went better with his shirt.

I'm starting to get irritated with him, and that's not how I want to feel when he proposes.

Taking a deep breath, I try to quell those thoughts and feelings but give maybe a little too much force to the frosting I'm mixing.

"Wow, what did that frosting do to you?" Mazie's voice catches me by surprise. I didn't know she'd be stopping by today.

"I'm just a little on edge."

"I can see that. Want to talk about it?"

"Cam told me he was going to propose. He hasn't yet. It's getting exhausting thinking he's going to every second of every day." I wipe the sweat from my brow as I continue to overwhip my frosting. I'm going to have to start again.

"Well, maybe he hasn't because you're waiting and expecting it."

My eyes lift to meet hers. "Yeah, that tends to happen when you're told about something."

She sighs heavily and rolls her eyes, tilting her head to the side in a true Mazie "are you an idiot" fashion. "What I mean is that Cam is probably picking up on that. He knows you're waiting and expecting, and for it to be a surprise, you need to stop."

"I don't know how to do that." I toss the bowl onto the counter and rest my hands against it, huffing some curls from my face. I'm supposed to be making an anniversary cake, but my mind is very much elsewhere.

"Try to let it go from your mind. He's waiting for a reason. Maybe there's something he's planned or something he's holding out for, but you have to know that you're just going to make yourself crazy."

"Oh, I've already done that." I look around the room at the chaos that is somewhat normal for cake decorating, but I know it's more. There's the pile of bowls with batter dripping down the sides that has to go in the trash because I forgot to add sugar. Sugar. A very basic and necessary ingredient in baking. And I forgot to add it.

"There's a difference between knowing it's going to happen and expecting it. Right now, it seems like you're expecting it at every turn instead of just waiting for it to happen. For all you know, it'll be months still. Does he even have a ring yet?" Leave it to Mazie to burst the bubble.

"I have no idea."

"That's a pretty big part of the process, Leen. He may be waiting for one to be ready or to go buy one."

I fall onto my stool. "Well, then why mention it? Why bring it up?"

"Did he?" She narrows her eyes at me, like she knows the answer but is trying to help me reach it. The only way she'd know is if Liv told her, which is entirely possible.

"Actually, no. I suppose I forced it out of him. He wanted to keep it a secret."

"Then I think you need to grant him a little grace and time. He's not ready just yet but will be. If he said he plans to, trust that, but don't expect it at every turn. Give him the time to make it right." She leans forward and runs her hand up and down my arm.

But I feel like I'm in a haze. I've just brought this nonsense upon myself. Yes, Cam may be exploiting it a bit by pretending he's going to propose and doing something else, but he didn't bring it up out of the blue. I made him tell me and now I'm letting it drive me mad.

"Are you okay with it, Maze? If Cam proposes?"

"I'm not your keeper, Alina. I'm your sister, and while it'd be nice for him to have talked to me or Eli, you don't need our permission." She squeezes my hand, and I meet her intent gaze.

"That's not what I mean. You haven't exactly been his biggest fan over the years." Possibly ever. We weren't exactly close when Cam and I started dating, so I don't know what she really thought of him then.

"Things are different now, Alina. He helped you in a time of crisis. You got the help you desperately needed, that I didn't know you needed, and he's responsible for that. It changes a lot of things and how I used to see him."

"Is it enough?"

"Are you happy?"

"Yeah. I really am. I love him and I know he loves me. I think Liv was right, that it's always been him."

"Then it's enough." Despite the hardships and nightmares, there are few times I've truly wanted Mom to be around. My first heartbreak, when Cam was MIA, when I didn't know how to break up with Sean. But this one is a topper.

"I miss them." I don't need to go into more detail.

"Me too, Leen. Every day. But I know they'd be proud of you, proud of us. We've done an amazing thing here. And look at Liv. Married, with a baby. I know it's been hard for her not having Mom around, but she's doing amazing." There's such awe in her voice and I can tell just by looking at her how proud she is of our baby sister, paving the way for both of us to come after.

"Liv's kind of amazing all on her own."

"She is. And I never gave her enough credit. It's something I'm trying to come to terms with, and at some point, I need to talk to her about."

"She knows. We both know you love us, Mazie. Sometimes you just take the mothering role too far. Because as much as you've stepped up and stepped in, you're not Mom and never will be." It's a harsh truth she needs to hear.

"I know." Her voice and head both drop, her curls forming a curtain on the side of her face.

"That's not a bad thing, Mazie. We *all* lost her. We don't need you to be her, we need you to be our sister. Especially now that we're all adults."

"Sometimes I don't know how to switch out of that role. It was important and something you needed when they first died. But now it's something I can't always push back." We've never had this open and honest of a conversation before, and it's refreshing.

"One thing I've learned in therapy is that once you're aware of it, you're more likely to be able to control it." Which I guess is advice for myself since now I can try to get myself to *stop* thinking about Cam proposing. It'll happen when it happens. That's my new mantra.

"I'll do my best. You know I'm only trying to look out for you guys, right?"

"I know. We both do, but it's overbearing at times." Really, most of the time, but I know she's coming from a good place, so I don't want to sound ungrateful. She's been an important aspect of our lives and helped us in many ways, even if sometimes she gets her roles backwards.

"Then I guess I'll just leave you with the thought of giving Cam some time and some grace. He loves you. It's been clear since he came to us about wanting to get you help for the nightmares. And if he hadn't left, then I'd say it's always been clear. That just makes it murky for me. But that's my own issue to get over." She holds her hand against her chest.

It's progress for Mazie to be able to not just accept but even acknowledge that Cam loves me. She's always been a little overly protective, even when Mom and Dad were still with us. But when they died, it kicked into overdrive. The only thing that makes me feel better about how much she hated Cam at first is that he deserved it, and she hated Jameson for no reason at all except that he was an outsider.

Now I just need to put the thoughts and actions into practice. I need to stop thinking about it, stop expecting it. He's made it clear he wants to propose, so I'm sure he will when he's ready and not a moment sooner. Besides, Mazie's right. Maybe he still needs to buy a ring. He said he wanted to and was planning something, which could absolutely include buying a ring.

I forced him to tell me; it wasn't something he just brought up out of the blue or started to propose but wasn't ready. He was keeping it a secret to surprise me, and I made him spill the beans.

This is on me, and I need to let it go and give him some more time to prepare and do what he plans.

I just hope he doesn't make me wait too long.

Chapter 36
Cameron

Having Mom's blessing to marry Alina means more than she could ever know. Or maybe she did and that's why she gave it before she passed.

I want Alina to have that too, but I can't ask her dad, much as I'd love to. He was a great man, from what I remember. Loved his family wholeheartedly and would do anything to keep his daughters safe and loved.

But there's one person he imparted that into. And it's Eli.

While at one point, we were like brothers, he was always hard on me, and that hasn't changed since I got back. Mazie and Liv both seem to have turned a corner, but I still get a lot of hard looks and a cold shoulder from Eli.

Part of it is the protectiveness he feels over his sisters, being not just the oldest, but the only brother. He knew Alina and I were intimate in our younger years, and it didn't sit right with him. The one time he pulled me aside to talk to me about it, he made that exceptionally clear, and that if anything happened, he'd hold me accountable.

Which is why I'm surprised he responded to my text at all. I stole his number from Alina's phone and sent him a message asking if we could chat. He agreed to meet me in Pineville City for a cup of coffee, which I know is so he doesn't have to be far from work or home, not to put in any extra effort, but I prefer it so Alina doesn't see us. There's only one decent place to get coffee in Juniper Grove.

Alina's been on edge since I told her I was planning to propose. It's like every instance she expects me to bend on one knee and pop the question. I may have exploited that a little bit and used it to have some fun, but I could tell it was starting to wear on her, so I stopped.

In recent days, she's seemed more relaxed so I'm hoping she hasn't given up that I'm still planning to.

Walking into the small coffee shop, I find Eli already in a chair, sipping from a yellow mug. He makes a face as he lowers the cup and pushes it a little farther away from himself. No coffee measures up to Three Sticks.

Irritation prickles up my spine. He shouldn't be here yet. I intentionally got here ten minutes early to beat him, to prove to him that I'm worthy.

Heaving a sigh, I head over with a smile on my face. "Hey, Eli. We said one, right?"

"I let my class go a little early to make sure I was here on time." He throws me a shit-eating grin, knowing he's getting under my skin by beating me here.

"Ah, well, thank you."

Though he nods, he says nothing, but I do catch him giving me a once-over as I sit across from him.

"Listen, man. We have history, and a strong one. At one point, I considered you like a brother to me. Even if you were always a little hard on me, I took it as brotherly love, and I know it was all out of love and protection of Alina. So I'm not going to beat around the bush here or bullshit you." I link my fingers in front of me and glance down at the tabletop while taking a sharp swallow.

After what feels like an eternity, I can meet his dark eyes again. "I want to propose to Alina. And I want your blessing."

His eyes widen for a brief moment before he puts a stoic face back on. "Why my blessing? I'm nobody important."

While I know for a fact Jameson asked permission as well, he wants me to recognize who he is to Alina, and not to boost his ego. He needs to make sure I understand the role he plays, the role they all play in one another's lives.

"You're the closest thing she has to a father figure. You're her big brother. And your opinion, your say, matters to her. Without it, I don't have a chance in hell."

That's when a wry smile crosses his face, and he leans forward. "Maybe I don't want you to have that chance." The thought has certainly crossed my mind.

"I can understand that. I was gone for a long time and left without a word. But that won't happen again."

"How do you know? How can you be so confident that you won't decide this isn't what you want anymore and split like last time? Or relapse?"

Chewing my lip, I process what to say, how best to answer him to calm his fears. They're completely rational fears for him to have. I'd expect the same questions from their father.

"I'm not a kid anymore, Eli. That was a long time ago. And part of the reason I never told Alina I was leaving was because if I went to her, I wouldn't have been able to go. I wouldn't have gotten the help I needed because I loved her too much. She doesn't know that, because I know she was already blaming herself, and none of it was her fault. But for me to just disappear in the middle of the night...it was the only way." I take a quick glance out the window and catch my reflection. So much more a man than I was at eighteen.

"I've been clean for ten years. There's nothing that can set me back, especially with Alina by my side. She's been instrumental in helping me stay clean after my mom passed. I won't lie, it was hard, and it hurts, you know that. But Alina sees me in a way nobody has ever cared to before and that has made all the difference. When we're married, when we have a family, there's nothing I'd do to risk even a second of time with her."

His eyes narrow and his tongue runs along his teeth as he takes me in. I'm not sure what he's going to say, if anything. For all I know, he's not going to give me an answer and instead will just stand and walk out.

After what feels like an eternity, Eli finally nods. "Okay. I give you my blessing." He points a finger in my direction, mere inches from my face. "Know one thing. If you break my sister's heart, I'm coming after you this time."

"Understood. I won't hurt her."

"You better not." He pauses and gives me another once-over. "Sheesh, the babies are growing up and getting married and having their own babies. Fuck, I'm an old shit," he mumbles more to himself than to me.

Silence surrounds us, and I link my fingers together on the table, not quite sure what to say now that I have his blessing but knowing he's still not a mega fan of mine. I'm on thin ice and high alert. This family won't give me more than an inch. Not that I really deserve it. Not yet, at least. I still have a lot of proving myself to do, and not just to Alina.

He doesn't let me wonder too long as he taps his fingers on the table and stands. "I have class to get back to."

"Wait, what? I thought you said you were free?"

"No, I said I *could* be free. And I was. For a short period of time. Besides, I had a feeling about what you wanted to talk about anyway. It's not like we're friends and you want to shoot the shit. It had to do with Alina, and I figured it was either this or something about her nightmares, so I wanted to be available either way." As he talks, he shrugs on a short wool coat. It's not really that cold out today, but I guess it adds to the professor look.

"Well, I guess I appreciate you making the time." I need to remember that this is Alina's brother, the closest thing she has to a father, and that he doesn't like me all that much. Rocking the boat isn't an option.

He claps me on the shoulder with a grin that tells me he knows he's being an asshole. To anybody else, it might seem sincere, but I've known Eli for too long to know it's nothing more than another shit-eating grin. "Any time."

After he leaves, I contemplate getting a cup of coffee, but remember Eli's face when he took a sip and decide it's probably better to pass.

This café has nothing for me. I have everything I came for.

Chapter 37
Alina

Getting my mind off of Cam proposing has been easier than I thought it would be. I really just put it out of my head and am living by the 'it will happen when it happens' mentality.

Chloe said it's just one more thing in my life that I can't control and need to be a bystander and wait. So, I'm doing my best.

Today's a day devoted solely to my sister and niece. I can't tell Liv, but I'm far more excited to see Jordanna than I am her. It's like something shifted the second I held that sweet baby girl in my arms, and now she's the main priority over my sister.

I'm sure Liv would agree, but she still likes to be the center of attention. Though I know she's the very middle of Jameson's universe.

With a deep breath, I let myself into her house. It's far different than it had been a mere month ago. At a little over ten weeks old, Jordanna is finally giving good naps and sleep. Liv has come back to the café a day here and there, and she seems like a new person. Highly refreshed from the new mom we saw not that long ago.

It's amazing what a little sleep can do for a person. I should know. It's been months since I've had a nightmare. While I can't say for certain, I think it's a combination of Cam's presence and the work I'm doing with Chloe.

At first, I had a few, dredging everything up again. But they've quieted as we've worked through the issues. The main one being that the incident with my parents was not my fault. Just because they were out that weekend instead of the one before like they'd planned before I got sick, doesn't mean things would have turned out differently.

For years, the nightmares came because I blamed myself for their death. Had I not gotten sick, had they not had to postpone their normal date night to a week later, maybe they'd still be alive.

But Chloe has made it clear I can't think that way. She also thinks I need to tell at least Liv my reasoning for thinking that. It's homework she's given me and something I plan to do today.

"Sibby?" As I make my way through the entryway and into the living room, Liv is nowhere to be found.

"In here!" her voice echoes from upstairs, and I know she's in Jordanna's room.

Within minutes, she's bounding down the stairs, a happy smiling baby cooing in her arms.

I lean in and give my sister a hug before scooping my niece right from her arms. Liv makes a face with one side of her mouth tipped down and puts her hands on her hips, but I know she's thankful for the break.

Jameson's been working with a vet's office near Pineville City for the past three weeks, so it's mostly been just Liv on her own.

"Well, hello, my absolutely perfect little niece. Hello." I tickle at her belly, and she smiles and coos, grabbing my finger and putting it in her mouth. Turning to face my sister, I move my upper half from side to side so Jordanna gets a bit of a rocking sensation.

"I'm sorry I won't be much entertainment for you today. But you said there was something you wanted to talk about?"

I give a sharp swallow before nodding. "Yeah, um, it's actually homework from Chloe."

She raises an eyebrow as she looks at me. "Therapists give homework?"

A giggle pulls from my chest. "Yes. I mean it's not like I'm being graded or anything but, I don't know, I like Chloe and working with her...it makes me want to do the things she suggests."

"Alright, well sit. Make yourself comfortable."

I follow her over to the sofa, where she sits against the arm, fiddling with her large diamond earring, and pulls her feet up under her.

I sit on the opposite end and use the arm to rest on to help me support Jordanna and her head. Babies are heavier than they seem when you're not used to holding one all the time.

As Jordanna gums my finger and moves it around with her tiny fist, I stare down at her perfection, proud of my sister and what she's accomplished, not just with her family, but in her life. She's a successful business owner, she has an extremely devoted husband, and by far the most adorable baby I've ever seen. She has her life together, and with the punches we were dealt, it would have been easy for her to fall off the wagon and not make much of herself.

"I'm proud of you, Liv."

"Thank you. I'm proud of you too, LeeLee. But that's not what you're here to tell me." Ah, Liv. Always so intuitive.

I smirk and glance at the floor, unable to meet her gaze. "So, Chloe wanted me to share what we think is the source of my nightmares."

When she doesn't respond, I lift my gaze and meet her wide purple eyes. I swear they've always seemed a shade of violet instead of blue. The pink has mostly faded from her hair, but I know she wants to do it again once Jordanna is a bit older. It's her signature style.

"One thing I've discovered with Chloe, that I'm not entirely sure I always understood, is that I blamed myself for their death."

A sharp intake of air is her only response.

I let the words linger until finally it becomes too much.

"Why? What on earth could possibly make you think it was your fault, Alina?"

"Remember they were supposed to go out the weekend before? But I got sick, and Mom insisted on staying home with me. Had I not been sick, had they gone the weekend before, maybe they wouldn't have gotten into that situation." There's a waver to my voice and an unmovable ache lodged in my throat.

Without a word, Liv practically throws herself across the couch and wraps her arms around my shoulders. "Oh, LeeLee. I had no idea you felt that way." As she leans back, she brushes some curls behind my shoulders. "None of it is your fault."

"While some part of me has always known that, it's also been hard to believe it. They were in a freak and horrifying event, with somebody who had lost his mind. But I just always felt like if I hadn't been sick, they wouldn't have gone the same weekend, and they would have avoided that particular person and that particular incident." My chin drops to my chest as a tear escapes.

Her hand squeezes mine, and I look up to meet her watery eyes. "I know it's hard to look at it any other way, and that it's hard to realize the falsehood of that thought process. But it could have happened for a million other reasons. They could have gone grocery shopping the same day, they could have gotten into an accident the weekend they were supposed to go out. There's no way of knowing what could have or would have happened, but assuming that they would still be alive...that's not something you can put on yourself or even pretend to know."

"I'm learning that. It's a slow and steady process, but I am learning."

"If I've come to realize one thing in my life, it's that everything happens for a reason. And I know it sounds incredibly cliché to say that, but it's true. Even the bad things." She scoots closer and runs her hand over Jordanna's head. The infant moves her eyes to find her mother and smiles widely.

"Losing Mom and Dad when we did, it helped shape who we are now. The lives we lead. Having Jordanna...I can't imagine my life being any different. And had they not died, I probably wouldn't be here, or married to Jameson, or have Jordanna." She chokes up at the end and I catch a tear sliding down her cheek.

"You can't know that, Liv." Though she probably wouldn't be anywhere near Juniper Grove.

"No, I do. Maybe by some off chance, I would have met Jameson somewhere, but it's highly unlikely. We were meant to lose them, as painful as it was and has been and continues to be. Do you know how often I want to pick up the phone to call Mom to ask her about something being normal or not? But I can't because she's not there. And I'm fine being the first to go through it. I'm okay with that. And I'm happy I'll be here for you and Mazie when you two finally decide to have kids, but it's *hard* and it hurts." The tears flow silently down her face.

"I know they would have made amazing grandparents, and it's hard that Jordanna will never get to know them. But we are who we are *because* we lost them. In spite of that great loss that could have derailed all of our futures, we've done pretty well for ourselves. Even Eli, who gave up more than we could have ever asked him to."

Every time Eli's sacrifices are mentioned, I feel like we need to give a moment of silence to mourn the life he should have had. Maybe the ones we all should have had. But Eli was on his way, living his life at MIT. The rest of us, well, things are just different than they maybe would have been.

"You would have moved to live in Manhattan. At least. If not California." A small smile pulls up the corner of my mouth, and when I glance at her, I notice a matching one on Liv's face.

"Oh, at least. I considered Europe for a while."

"Anywhere but here," we both murmur together.

"I'm glad you stayed, Sibby. Because you absolutely still could have left and lived your dreams."

"No, I couldn't have. After they died, we needed to stay together. And as much as I hate to admit it, Juniper Grove is home. Now it always will be." The thought of Liv raising Jordanna here makes my heart happy. The fact that our kids will all be as close as we are.

"Oh, let me take her?" I glance down at the infant in my arms who's starting to squirm. She's been so quiet I almost thought she fell asleep.

Instead of handing her over, I turn myself to the side to keep her away from Liv. "What? Why? It's my time with her."

"She's rooting. She's hungry." Liv holds her hands out and waggles her fingers toward her body.

"I'm sorry, she's what?"

"Rooting. It means she's looking around for a boob and, sorry, but yours just won't do." Without giving me a second to comprehend, she scoops Jordanna and smiles down at her, lifting her shirt and pulling out her breast, which the infant immediately latches on to.

"I'm proud of you, Sibby. You're an amazing mom so far. And I'm sure it's hard without advice from friends and family."

"Thanks, LeeLee. It's been a learning curve, for sure. But we're getting the hang of it. Aren't we?" She runs a finger up Jordanna's cheek, and she closes her tiny fist around it as she eats.

"Alright. I think I'm going to leave you to it." I pat my knees and stand, ready to let them enjoy their alone time. Especially because I see Jordanna's eyes drifting shut.

"No, stay. She's going to fall asleep any minute, and then we can have some time to chat."

"Everything I needed to say, I did. I don't want to be in your hair too much. Besides, if she sleeps, you should too." That's what everybody says, right? Is that less true now that she's a little older?

"Now that she sleeps better, I'm not *as* exhausted, but a nap does sound wonderful. Thank you for coming by, Alina. And thank you for sharing with me. I think it'd be good for you to talk to Mazie and Eli too, but I can understand that it's hard to talk about." Liv has always understood far outside what she's told.

"In good time. It's not even something I've shared with Cam yet. It kind of just erupted from me one day in therapy, and Chloe said I needed to share with a family member, somebody I'm close to, and you were the only option for that." I smile at her, my amazing little sister.

Leaning across the couch, I pull her in for a hug and give Jordanna's tiny foot a squeeze. While she's fallen asleep, she's still attached to Liv.

"I love you, Sibby." I run a hand down her curls.

"Love you too, LeeLee."

As I leave the house, I feel lighter and looser, like I've finally released a tension that was holding me taut at all times. There's weight lifted from my body, all of it. It's like I can breathe easier, walk easier, and simply exist easier now than I have in years.

I knew Liv wasn't going to blame me, that was never a concern. But I was worried that maybe she'd agree with and understand my thought process. Which I suppose is, in a way, blaming me anyway. But she didn't. She refuted my thoughts, my fears, and that makes everything better.

Imagine how light I'll feel when I've also talked to Cam, Mazie, and Eli. I worry I might float away on the next breeze.

Chapter 38

Cameron

"Thanks for letting me in, Mazie. I know it's not somewhere I should be." She's helping me set out candles around the kitchen at the café.

The smell of cake wafts through my nose, but it's far less sweet and delicious than Alina's. I hope I didn't fuck this up too terribly.

"Of course, Cam. I think this is the perfect spot. She'll be back soon, though. Liv texted me that she left."

"Well, then I guess you should get out of here. Thanks again."

With a curt nod, Mazie lets herself through the door.

I take a deep breath to try to calm my racing heart. This is it. The moment I've been waiting for. I was thankful Liv was willing to help out and invite Alina over for a couple of hours. It gave me time to bake this probably atrocious cake and put out the candles, all of which are now lit.

My heart stops as I hear the door shut.

"Cam?"

Turning around, I find Alina with her keys in one hand, head cocked to the side. "What's going on here?"

I walk over to her and wrap my arm around her waist, taking her keys from her hand and setting them on the closest surface. "Hi. How was your day with Liv?"

"It was good. Cathartic. Something that I needed."

A smile pulls at my lips. She's in a good mood. "That's great."

With my hand behind her back, I lead her over to the center counter where I have my concoction. "I baked you something."

Her face falters for a moment as she looks at the messy and dripping frosting. "It looks great." She looks up at me with a beaming smile.

"It looks like shit. But hopefully it doesn't taste like it."

Taking a large knife, I cut a slice and give it to her. Hesitantly, she grabs a fork and digs in.

And immediately starts coughing.

I quickly grab her a glass of water and a napkin. "That bad?"

"It's just a little dry." She states after a gulp of water.

"Sorry. Definitely not the baker here." I sigh heavily. "I just wanted to do something special for you and I felt like cake is something you bake every day, but how often do you have a cake baked for you?"

She touches her hand to her chest and then to mine, pushing up onto her toes to kiss my cheek. "Thank you. It's very sweet. And you're right, nobody ever bakes for me."

"I was going to write on it with frosting, but that was just a mess. You can see here," I pause to point to the top left corner where there's some smudged blue, "where I attempted it before wiping it off."

"That's okay. It's the thought that counts."

I run a hand down my face as my heart thumps erratically. "I'm fucking this all up. I wanted it to say, 'will you marry me.' And I even thought about hiding the ring in the cake but then I was worried you wouldn't be able to find it. And I just—"

She puts her hand on my jaw and stops me. "Sorry. Say that again? You wanted the cake to say what?" There's a glistening in her eyes as the candlelight bounces off them.

This is the moment I have to get right. So, I take the plate from her hands and bend on one knee. "I love you, Alina. I've always loved you. And I'm sorry I was gone for so long because we could have had so much more together. But let's have it now. Let's make up for lost time and do and have all the things we always wanted. Marry me? Please?"

She starts nodding slowly, then faster and faster. "Yes, Cam. Of course, I'll marry you."

With a smile so wide it hurts my jaw, I pull the ring from my pocket and slip it on Alina's finger. It fits perfectly.

Her eyes glisten and widen as she eyes the ring. She pulls me to stand and crashes against my chest, taking my face between her palms to collide my mouth against hers.

My arms wrap around her waist, and I tug her against me, my tongue slipping between her lips.

The most amazing woman in the world just agreed to marry me. I'm such a fuck up, I definitely don't deserve her, but I'll spend the rest of my life doing whatever I can to try.

Epilogue
Alina

C am officially moved into my house two weeks ago. Though he'd basically been living here since coming back for his mom, it's official now. We went to his apartment and cleared out his belongings and signed the papers to give up his holding. We had to wait until his lease was up, which took four months from him proposing.

It wasn't a bad thing, though, because it meant he could go to more meetings. Instead of driving back, he'd stay the night at his apartment. Sometimes I'd go with him and spend the time at a local shop while he had his meeting. It's something we do together.

My hours at the café have changed drastically. It's easier now that I have something else to occupy my time. Or I suppose someone else. Not to mention the need to distract my mind from racing thoughts is nowhere near as prevalent as it used to be.

While I still do all of the baking both for the café and any side jobs, I schedule my hours very differently. I'm still up and in early, with Cam in tow, but tend to finish before five and meet Cam at home for dinner.

The time we spend together is something I've come to cherish. Not just because I love him, but it's in those moments that we're alone that we're the most vulnerable with each other.

When I told him about feeling guilty for how my parents died, he hugged me so tightly I could barely breathe. Then he covered me in words and whispers of affirmations and that he loves me. He apologized for being gone, sure that if he had stayed, I wouldn't have gone so long thinking it was my fault.

Being home alone allows for that rawness that being at the café never seemed to, even though we were always alone.

"Ali?" Cam's voice echoes through the house.

"Kitchen!" I give an absentminded stir to the vegetables in the pan on the stove.

He wraps his arms around my waist and bends to kiss my neck. While he mostly works from his phone, he's taken to getting some work done at his dad's house to be sure he's around enough and supportive in his dad's rough time.

"Mmm, that smells delicious."

"Thank you." While he's offered to cook, especially on days that he's working from home instead of his dad's, I enjoy it too much to let it go. It allows me to destress and relax after the day. Though I don't find the day-to-day baking stressful, the time frame which I give myself can set me a little on edge. Not to mention, the stakes of messing something up.

But making dinner allows me to just focus on one task and enjoy a nice glass of wine while I do so.

With a quick bite to my shoulder, he backs away and rummages in the fridge for a beer. Every now and again, he'll join me with a drink. It's something that he takes seriously, not overdoing it. But he trusts that he can have one now and again and not fall down the rabbit hole, and I trust him to know his limits.

It took a bit for me to get to that point, of knowing I could trust him. But every day he shows me how strong he is. He communicates openly and honestly.

We check in every few days for both of us. How we're feeling, how things are going, if there's anything we need to talk about. It's how I brought up my guilt. Chloe called it survivor's guilt. Even though I wasn't in the car, it's still something I've felt because I was left behind.

As the time creeps by from his mom passing, Cam's felt both better and worse. Sometimes, he feels worse after realizing he's had a good stretch of days and hasn't thought about her much. It's caused him to want to attend weekly meetings again.

It's also hard with the wedding coming up. Neither of us have said it out loud, but between the two of us, we'll have one parent in attendance. It's heavy in many ways, and while we don't vocalize it, we can each feel the weight of it as we plan.

There are things we tiptoe around, words we don't say, and parts of normal weddings that we don't even bring up for ours. Such as the father-daughter and mother-son dances. We know we won't be having those, so we skip right past them.

"What's on the agenda tonight?" He leans against the counter next to me and takes a swig from his beer.

"I was thinking we take it easy and watch a show or movie."

"You sure? I know we have a lot to plan, and things are coming up soon." We decided not to wait too long. Not only do we not see a reason, but we don't have a huge number of people to invite. We have a justice of the peace coming out to us at Liv's house where she's graciously offered to host in her backyard.

It's similar in feel to Liv's. Small and intimate. Between the two of us, we don't have much family to speak of. My siblings, his dad, and a small smattering of cousins on his side, not that he's close with them.

While Cam has a small group of friends and group members he'd like to invite, I don't really have many friends. It makes the tiny setting feel all the more special.

"Yeah, I'm sure. I want a night just us hanging out and not having the wedding looming over us. We've dealt with a lot of details already."

"You sure you still want to make the cake?" He cocks an eyebrow as he dips his head.

"I'm the best cake baker in the area. I'm not going to pay somebody to do what I can. Besides, I can make it beforehand and not have to really worry about it on the day of. It's not the same as cooking." That was an argument that I had to give a little for. Cam didn't feel I should be the one cooking on our special day and that the food should be fresh, not prepared the day before.

He's right, of course, but it was hard to give in. Instead, we're getting it catered by a local Italian restaurant that I actually like.

The whole thing has come together nicely, even if we still have a few things to do. Cam has entrusted me to make the cake, despite still feeling as though I should let somebody else handle it.

Liv and Jameson are, of course, handling the location, and their gift to us is hiring somebody to come out and decorate.

"And you're sure you're okay having a small wedding? Not the big fairy tale thing girls dream about." He asks this question about three times a day.

I know he's just concerned that I'm going to have regrets. Setting my wine down, I put the wooden spoon on the edge of the pan and flip off the burner so I can turn to Cam and wrap my arms around his neck.

"It's not the wedding I dreamed about when I was a little girl. But that's okay, because things aren't the way they were when I was little. This is going to be perfect. Besides, none of it really matters. I'm just happy I get to marry you." I push up onto my toes and connect my lips with his.

His gaze penetrates mine as he loops a curl around my ear. "I just want you to be happy."

"I am. And I will be. I don't need a fancy dress or venue or anything to make me happy. Just you."

"You're still getting the dress, though, right?"

It's been another topic of contention. Backyard doesn't scream fancy dress to me, and I'm fine finding more of a sundress. But Cam and my sisters insist that I need a real and fancy wedding dress because I'll only be married once.

"Yes. I'm still getting the dress. I'm going with Mazie and Liv next weekend to check out a few stores." I lower to my feet and switch back to cooking our ratatouille.

It's very natural, cooking with Cam and having him home for dinner. It feels right.

Cam was somebody I didn't realize I was missing until he returned, and it scared the shit out of me when he did.

But I know that he was a piece of me that was always supposed to be here. A piece of self that he had taken with him a long time ago that only returned once he came back into my life.

Now that he's back and we're together, I'm finally whole again.

Epilogue
Cameron

The party's in full swing, and everybody seems to be having a wonderful time. Alina looks stunning in her sheath dress, and I feel like a penguin in my tux. But I'm finally a married man and to the girl of my dreams.

Standing off to the side, I watch as Alina dances with Liv, glass of champagne in her hand, and can't help but smile.

"You look like a happily married man, and it's only been an hour." Eli sidles up next to me and takes a drink of what smells like scotch.

"What can I say? Your sister makes me happy beyond what I ever dreamed was possible and certainly beyond what I deserve."

"I won't deny that. My sisters are too good for any of the men in their lives. Including me." He takes another stiff sip and pockets his other hand.

"Thank you for helping out with the wedding. I know it's probably not what anybody anticipated, but Alina seems happy, and that's all I care about."

"I'm on the same page with you. If she's happy, that's all I care about." We're both watching the sisters dance together on the makeshift dance floor.

Jameson was able to find a company that brings out and assembles a dance floor in your yard, then comes back and takes it away. He's a pretty generous guy, and I can't wait to get to know him more. While we've had our interactions and moments, things became harder once Jordanna was born. But as she's gotten older, they've been able to do more again. At the very least, I owe him a drink for letting me have my wedding at his mansion.

We continue to shoot the shit for a few minutes, when I hear some commotion behind us. Turning around, I find none other than Zach stumbling sideways and knocking over chairs as he makes a beeline for what looks like the dance floor and the girls.

Eli and I both stand straighter and head over to intercept him.

"Whoa, buddy. Hey, what's going on?" Eli puts his hands on Zach's shoulders and stops him while I cross my arms against my chest.

"I have to tell her." He's slurring his words. I don't know how the bartender let him get so sloshed. Besides, he's a cop, shouldn't he keep his wits about him a little more?

Or maybe he's off the clock and decided to let loose.

"Tell who what?" I try to be gentle, but I'm not feeling all that giving at the moment.

"Mazie."

Eli looks over at me with wide eyes, and we both know that he's going to do something he'll regret in the morning, along with the massive hangover he's going to have.

"What do you need to tell her?" Though Eli pushes, I think we both know what he wants to say.

"That I love her. That I've always loved her. It's always been her, and she just sees me as a friend, but I'm so much more than that. I have to be more than that. Can't I be more than that?" Zach tips a bit to the side, and Eli grabs him to straighten him up.

"Instead of telling Mazie right now, why don't we let her enjoy the dance with her sisters and get you some coffee."

"Mazie!" Instead of listening to Eli, Zach tries to yell over the music.

Eli and I make eye contact again as Eli shoves Zach into a chair at one of the tables. He waves his hand to call over one of the waitstaff who have been asked to circle through the evening.

"We need coffee. Right now." I get right to the point.

"Yes, sir." The waiter backs away immediately.

"I love you! I'm in love with you!" Though Zach's shouting, I doubt he can be heard over the music.

"Alright, buddy. Now's not the best time to tell her that. We're at Alina and Cam's wedding. We don't want to take the spotlight away from them, do we?" Eli's tone is gentle, like he's talking to a child, which I guess isn't all that different from talking to a drunk person.

"No. No, I'm sorry." He turns to me and puts a heavy hand on my shoulder. I'm not entirely sure why he wanted to come in the first place. He's never been a fan of mine, and when I was using, I avoided him. Like he'd be able to smell it on me or something. But he's Mazie's plus one and basically part of the family.

"I just love her and seeing her sisters get married. She needs to know. I have to tell her." There's a waver to his voice, and I wonder if he's going to cry.

"How about you wait until tomorrow when Mazie's done having fun with her sisters. Look at them, they're all smiling and having a great time."

I glance behind me and see what Eli's talking about. The three of them are huddled together with their faces tipped toward the sky as they sing the lyrics to the 90s pop hit.

"You're right, Eli. You're always so smart. So smart. I'll tell her tomorrow." Without another word, he puts his head on the table and falls asleep.

"He's going to pay for this in the morning."

"Oh, absolutely. Thanks for intervening. Not sure how that works with somebody professing their feelings during the sister's wedding." I glance toward the girls one more time to find them laughing, and a smile pulls up the corner of my mouth.

This was the only possible hiccup on an otherwise perfect day.

The only question is whether he's going to tell Mazie or not. And how she'll react when she finally hears what we've all always known.

The End
Mazie's story comes next!

COMING October 2023

The following is an unedited preview and subject to change.

Chapter 1

M azie

How did this happen? How did they surpass me in life?

As I dance and sing at the top of my lungs with my baby sisters at Alina's wedding, those questions keep circling in the back of my mind. I can't believe they're both married now. And Liv has a baby. It doesn't even feel real.

It's not that I'm jealous. Well, not entirely. How could I not be when I so desperately want to be a wife and mother? But I'm not angry jealous. I love them both dearly and I'm incredibly happy for them finding their perfect matches, finding their forevers.

But I'd be lying if I said I wasn't a little sad for me.

The free-flowing alcohol helps numb the sting a little bit. As does this carefree moment with our arms around each other as we scream-sing a song from when we were younger.

There is a sadness weighing me down, but it has nothing to do with my sisters passing me in life's accomplishments and everything to do with who's missing.

Our parents.

They would have been over the moon at each wedding and the most doting grandparents the world has ever seen for Liv's baby. I can hear Mom now, calling Jordanna her baby's baby.

It's not often that I think about how unfair life has been to me and my siblings by tearing them away from us, and so brutally. But the thought has been on my mind more lately.

Especially for Liv. She had the least time with them, the least time to get Mom's sage advice and Dad's handy skills. The least fatherly protection and motherly love.

It's where my brother, Eli and I have stepped in the best we could. It wasn't even a conscious decision; we knew what had to be done and got to it. I know I overstep my bounds sometimes, but I'm a worrier at heart.

Their murder made it hard for me to trust people. It's why I gave Jameson such a hard time at first. He's an outsider, and I don't like opening our family to outsiders. In fact, I don't really like outsiders at all. Which is a large reason I tend to do most of my work for the café from home.

It's also probably why Zach is my best friend. We've known each other since we were kids. He's not just a good person, but he's a safe place for me too.

And that's probably how I pick his voice out above the music. He's urgently trying to express something, but what, I can't tell. Concern takes over the fun, and I hope he's okay. I saw him downing drink after drink. Not something he does often, since he rarely takes a day off from work.

As the song ends and changes to something a little slower, I make my way toward the tables and find him seated with Eli and Cameron, both shoulder to shoulder in front of him.

I walk over to them and push them apart as a waiter brings over a cup of steaming coffee.

Kneeling in front of Zach, I put my hands on his to get him to look at me. But instead, he sways slightly, a stupid smirk on his face. He's three sheets to the wind.

"Mazie! There she is." The words come out way too loud and a bit slurred. His eyes are red and glossy.

"Hey, Zach. What's going on?" I try to make my voice sound as calming as possible, even when I'm borderline panicked. I don't know what to do with a drunken Zach. While I've seen it several times over the course of our friendship, it's been years and he's far bulkier than he ever was back in high school and college.

"I had a few drinks. They were so good. And I have to tell you that I—"

"He wanted to tell you that he was having a great time and that you look beautiful," Eli interjects while clapping a hand on Zach's shoulder at the same time that Cameron shoves the coffee into Zach's hands.

My eyes narrow, and I know they're hiding something, but I don't push, not wanting to start anything at my sister's wedding.

Standing, I turn around and lean into Eli. "You're going to have to help me get him home. You know that, right?"

"Yup. Already figuring out if we should let him hang here or try to get him out sooner as opposed to later."

I glance over my shoulder to take another look at Zach's condition. "Let's see how the coffee treats him. But he needs a babysitter."

"You or me?"

"If you don't mind, I'm going to ask you, because if he falls, I can't catch him."

"I'm not sure I can either. He's a big dude." While Eli has some muscles himself, Zach is broad, with muscles on muscles. While it's not usually my thing, I've always felt like it suits Zach.

And I can't deny how safe I feel with him, and not just because he's a cop. He could pummel anybody who tried to hurt me. There's certainly been a time or two he's wanted to when some guy I was dating broke my heart. Most can't handle the dead parents and how that has come to affect me on a daily basis. Such as the crippling anxiety I just can't rid myself of.

But Zach was there through it all. He lets me be me. That's why he's such an amazing friend, and I'm so lucky to have him.

Turning back to check on Zach again, I find him passed out on the table, mouth open and surely snoring. I've always promised not to tell any future girlfriends that the man snores like a Mac truck roaring down the highway.

"I think he'll be okay for a while. If you don't mind sitting with him? Just in case he wakes up." I bite my lip and raise my eyebrows toward Eli. I already know he'll say yes. He's a good man and a better brother. But I still feel guilty asking since it's his sister's wedding too.

"Not a problem. You know I'm not much for dancing anyway. Plus, you girls looked like you were having fun."

I notice that Liv and Alina are still on the dance floor, and a smile pulls up the corners of my lips. "Yeah. We were."

Things have been tense, off and on, over the past...well...several years, really. But especially when Jameson came into Liv's life. And again, when Cam was first back. That motherly role hasn't gone away just because they're adults. They still don't have Mom around and I feel like I need to be there in whatever way I can be.

It's nice for us to have this time together when the stressors of life and things that have been said or done are far behind us.

Because the first time one of the bonehead brothers-in-law messes up, I'll be the first to jump to my sister's defense.

Acknowledgments

W hat an amazing journey it's been to get here. With that, comes many thanks.

To my amazing husband and children:

Another book, another thank you. I still cannot begin to truly show or explain my gratitude for all that you do and all the ways you continue to support me on this incredible journey.

I truly could not do a single aspect of this without you. Having you by my side every step of the way means so much to me.

I love you!

To my amazing duo; AK, RL:

You are my rock solid team. There for any question, any confusion, any help I need, I know you're there. It's amazing to have found not just great writing partners, but friends.

To my awesome beta readers:

Thank you so much for coming on late in the game. And especially for loving this story as much as I do! You've been so helpful and I can't wait to share more work with you.

To my incredible street team:

Thank you all for you continued support of me and my work. It's amazing to have readers who enjoy my work enough to want to promote it for others to read. I'm truly thankful for you all.

To my amazing editors Mackenzie and Beth:

This book would not be what it is without you and your input. Thank you for helping me learn how to be a better writer, adjusting my words, and most importantly, keeping my voice my own. And especially for your beautiful words as you read through it.

Thank you to the amazing **Fine's Fine Designs** for my stunning cover!

To my ARC team: Your time and effort does not go unnoticed. Thank you for reading my novel before it hit the public and for your gracious reviews. I know it's not always easy to find the words, but it's all so appreciated.

And most importantly, to the readers:

Thank you for taking a chance on a small author like myself. I know it can be difficult to see a new name and say "hey let me try that" but it is so beyond appreciated, I cannot begin to find the words. I write because it's my passion, but I publish because I want to share my words with all of you. I hope you enjoyed reading it, as much as I enjoyed writing it.

About the Author

S hayna Astor is a romance author who loves writing sweet love stories, with a lot of spice. When she's not writing, she's probably watching The Office with a cup of coffee, spending time with her kids, or playing video games with her husband.

Stalk me for all the latest updates, teasers for upcoming novels, give-aways, and all the goods on what's coming next!

Instagram @shayna.astor.author

TikTok @shayna.astor.author

Facebook Group Shayna's Coffee Corner

Website www.shaynaastor.com

www.ingramcontent.com/pod-product-compliance
Lightning Source LLC
Chambersburg PA
CBHW030656260626
47157CB00007B/2673